0 026 462 28X 16

KT-387-790

Head

Jill Marshall moved from the United Kingdom to New Zealand, along with her small daughter and her even smaller mad dog. Her childhood ambition was to become an author, so in 2001 Jill gave up her career at a huge international company to concentrate on writing for children. When not working, writing and being a mum, Jill plays guitar, takes singing lessons and is learning to play the drum kit she has set up in the garage. One day she might even sing in a band again . . .

SE

A fine will .

Also by Jill Marshall

Jane Blonde, Sensational Spylet*
Jane Blonde Spies Trouble
Jane Blonde, Twice the Spylet
Jane Blonde, Spylet on Ice
Jane Blonde, Goldenspy
Jane Blonde, Spy in the Sky
Jane Blonde, Spylets are Forever

* Also available in audio

JILL MARSHALL

SEFTON LIBRARY SERVICES	
002646228	
Bertrams	26/08/2009
JF	3
	£5.99

First published 2009 by Macmillan Children's Books
a division of Macmillan Publishers Limited
20 New Wharf Road, London N1 9RR
Basingstoke and Oxford
Associated companies throughout the world
www.panmacmillan.com

ISBN 978-0-330-45153-6

Copyright © Jill Marshall 2009

The right of Jill Marshall to be identified as the
author of this work has been asserted by her in accordance
with the Copyright, Designs and Patents Act 1988.

All rights reserved. No part of this publication may be
reproduced, stored in or introduced into a retrieval system, or
transmitted, in any form or by any means (electronic, mechanical,
photocopying, recording or otherwise), without the prior written
permission of the publisher. Any person who does any unauthorized
act in relation to this publication may be liable to criminal
prosecution and civil claims for damages.

1 3 5 7 9 8 6 4 2

A CIP catalogue record for this book is available from
the British Library.

Typeset by Nigel Hazle
Printed and bound in the UK by CPI Mackays, Chatham ME5 8TD

This book is sold subject to the condition that it shall not,
by way of trade or otherwise, be lent, resold, hired out,
or otherwise circulated without the publisher's prior consent
in any form of binding or cover other than that in which
it is published and without a similar condition including this
condition being imposed on the subsequent purchaser.

For Christopher Roberts.
About time I gave you a proper book to read x

1

EGYPT, 1922

The preparation was just as it should be. Painstaking. Immaculate. It had to be, to have any chance of fending off what had been unleashed. The young man patted his pocket, just to assure himself that the letters were there. Then, with a deep breath, he picked up his instruments and set about the body.

First the brain, chopped up inside the head and, with a long hook, withdrawn in pieces through the nostril. The wobbling grey mass was discarded into a bucket, like the guts of a fish. There would be no need for it now.

Not so the other organs. They were carefully withdrawn and stored in their little jars, to be watched over for all eternity by the figureheads attached to the lids of the stone urns: the stomach, guarded by Duamutef; the lungs, nestled under the baboon head of Hapy; the intestines in the jar beneath Qebehsenuef of the falcon head. The only

1

human-headed god of the four, Imsety, sat aloft and imperious, not minding that the intestines of an expired human swam in gore and untold filth in the jar beneath it.

The person performing the organ removal minded though. The stench was unbearable. The gods alone knew what the corpse beneath his hands had eaten last. Curried goat, perhaps, or something French steeped in garlic. The other man's eating habits had changed rather a lot recently, since meeting the girl. 'Good Lord, Jay – couldn't you stick to bread and cheese like the rest of us?' he hissed, retching, eyeing the bucket before averting his eyes quickly from the jellied brains and pulling himself back into the moment. Through gritted teeth the man muttered in a low chant as he sealed the jars closed with a candle . . . 'I am the horned bull who rules the sky, Lord of Celestial Appearings, the Great Illuminator who came forth from the heat . . . I detest what is detestable. I will not eat faeces. I will not drink urine. I will not walk head downward . . .'

The jars were placed alongside the body. 'I am loosed from my windings,' continued the man, pulling his spectacles further down his nose to focus as he turned his attention to the most important part of the process. 'I make ready the ferry boat of the sky; I eat of what they eat, I live on what they live, I have eaten bread in every pleasant room.'

Swallowing back the rising tide of nausea, the temporary surgeon picked up the golden beetle from the table. The scarab would protect the heart, the most vital of all the body parts, the only organ to remain inside the body. It was the critical piece in the final judgement, without which there could be no balance, no passing through . . .

The surgeon moved aside the corpse's crossed hands, exposing the linen that covered the heart, ready to lay the golden amulet upon it. But just as he was about to lower the great scarab there was a commotion at the far end of the tunnel, followed swiftly by a dull explosion. Dust billowed into the room, snuffing out the candles, and then what the surgeon had dreaded all along.

He – it – was coming.

Staggering from the awful realization and the aftershocks of the explosion, the man only just managed to refrain from grabbing the side of the coffin and toppling it to the floor. The golden scarab slid off the corpse's chest, landing near the surgeon's outstretched hand. It gave him an idea. Only one thing could save his master now.

A green aura, the fetid breath of a long-dead spirit, was thickening in the gloom along the tunnel, fogging the entrance. Soon the whole crypt would be plunged into darkness.

Time had run out. He had to act. Now.

The young man raised his scalpel. 'Forgive me, my friend,' he whispered, and he plunged the glittering blade into his master's chest, thanking his own gods that the heart he was about to plunder was no longer beating.

2

Jack Bootle-Cadogan cleared his throat. Speaking in public was one of those things he would have to get used to when he became lord of all he surveyed, etcetera and la-di-da and all that. But just now he felt like a boy, a very young boy of not quite thirteen (which was actually, when it came down to it, still only twelve). And the weight of the day was enormous, with all those faces turned towards him expectantly, some streaked with tears, others a little worried – perhaps on his behalf, or perhaps about what he might say . . .

'Erm, my great-grandmother Granny Dazzle,' he started, reaching for his handkerchief in case he blubbed and made a complete idiot of himself, 'was quite an extraordinary person.'

A few nods. Nobody could disagree with that. His mother was even patting his father on the knee in a comforting fashion.

Feeling a little braver, Jack took a deep breath.

'I mean, not many people get to live until they're a hundred and three.' There were more nods, and Jack relaxed. 'That's right – a hundred and three. Born before there were even cars on the roads. Imagine that! And up until last year she was still sneaking out secretly at midnight to go drinking, betting on the horses, dancing on tables and . . . oh.'

Lady Bootle-Cadogan, Jack's mother, was shaking her head vigorously, staring hard at the Bible she clutched in her hand. Of course. Nobody else needed to know about that. Even Granny had done a good job of hiding it all. Jack searched for some safer ground.

'OK, well, I talked a lot to Granny Dazzle – sorry, Lady Diselda – in the last few months. All through my life really. She was a very good friend to me. An unusual friend, it's true, because she was sort of . . . well, wrinkly – really wrinkly – and with kind of a funny smell. A bit like a cat-litter tray. But still a really, really good friend. And one thing she always told me was that we mustn't be sad when she died. Because . . .' The lump in his throat seemed to swell in size and he swallowed hard. 'Because she wouldn't be sad herself. She'd be with her beloved Jay again, and that was all that mattered. She'd have the marriage that was snatched from her when she was much, much too young.'

Jack paused to sniffle a little. She'd meant every word, of course. For months before she faded away completely she'd been digging out sepia-tinted newspaper articles, making him read them aloud to her, over and over, never tiring or growing bored of them, even though Jack certainly did after the fortieth or fiftieth reading. Even articles like LORD BOOTLE-CADOGAN UNEARTHS HIDDEN TOMB palled after a while, although the photos were still wonderful to him: his tall, mustachioed great-grandfather supervising the removal of a sarcophagus, aided by his young companion from the Bootle-Cadogan estate, Albert Cornthwaite, thin and bookish and slightly mole-like, finally managing to break a smile as he watched the stone tomb swing on its ropes against the backdrop of Syrian sand dunes.

The other clippings were in Jack's hand now, burning against his palm. He'd meant to put them in the coffin with Granny Dazzle but had arrived too late, after it was sealed. He'd have to put them in a scrapbook or something. DISELDA THE DANCING DARLING ENSNARES BRITAIN'S MOST ELIGIBLE

BACHELOR – that was when Lord Jay and she first met, when the outrageous Diselda Carruthers draped her locket around the neck of the handsome young man in the audience in Cairo, whispering, 'And now you have my heart on a string,' into his ear; SHOCK MARRIAGE – the words forming an umbrella over the image of his young and beautiful great-grandmother in a slender sheath of white silk, her head weighed down by one of her enormous feather headbands, and Lord Jay's moustache turned upwards at each corner by the great toothy spread of his smile; and the saddest of all: BOOTLE-CADOGAN DIES FROM SCORPION BITE. It was dated just a month after their wedding. Mere weeks after the greatest discovery of the modern age. And swathed and swaddled for ever after in deep suspicion and myths.

'There was always talk of a curse, of course – mummies and diseases and that type of lunacy,' Granny Dazzle would tell Jack with a smile, watching him carefully to make sure he wasn't alarmed. 'I was even told by a beggar woman at the excavation site that the necklace she sold me would protect me and my offspring from the wrath of Seth, right until the day I die.'

'Who's Seth? Lord Jay's rival?' Jack had asked.

'Goodness, no! Seth was some Ancient Egyptian god. Rather nasty, by all accounts, and in the habit of cursing people. But what rot, Jack! The only curse Jay ever fell under was his wretched need for adventure. Which, of course, was why I loved him so.'

Someone coughed gently. How long had he been standing there silently, immersed in his memories? His parents were holding their breath, he could see. Probably wondering if he was going to pass out. Or run. Or completely let the side down and crash to his knees, wracked with great gulping sobs. With a tiny sniff so that everyone would think he'd simply been having a quiet yet dignified weep to himself, he lifted his head and pointed his long, aristocratic nose towards the congregation.

'Anyway, you all already know about my lovely great-granny so I'll shut up now,' he said, and he dipped underneath the coffin to pull out a large ghetto blaster. 'And you can blame her for this.' He pressed the play button and stood well back, suddenly grateful that the chapel didn't have an organ. Otherwise she'd have had him in his tailcoat, hammering away at the keys like the Phantom of the Opera or something. 'Sorry, everyone.

But she insisted we mustn't be sad. And this is the song she wanted.'

And from the stone steps at the altar of the Bootle-Cadogan family chapel came the tinny voice of Barry Manilow singing *Copacabana*.

Jack shrugged as many members of the congregation laughed, and a few, his mother included, gasped in horror. The song suited Granny Dazzle like no other. A showgirl to the end. With a brief nod towards the closed coffin, he strode away down the aisle. He'd done his bit. It was time to let her go.

As he reached the heavy oak door he suddenly felt a bit shaky, and it was only then that he remembered what he was. Not a lord-in-the-making. Just a kid really, who'd lost his beloved great-grandmother. He sat down abruptly on one of the bench seats in the chapel's little entrance hall and put his head in his hands, letting loose a few timely bellows of pain, finally releasing all the emotion he'd been carefully bottling up for the last six days . . . until a strange sound made him look up.

Someone else crying? No. It was a bleat! Some sheep was bah-ing its head off nearby. But there was no working farm on the estate any more, and no other livestock anywhere within a twenty-mile radius – as far as the estate stretched, in fact.

But there was a sheep, right outside the church – and a couple of goats. They were all tethered to a tree on the other side of the fence, away from the chapel. It was Granny Dazzle's special tree – the Egyptian tamarisk tree she had planted after Lord Jay died and she took up residency as Lady Bootle-Cadogan, much to his family's disgust. As she was pregnant with the future Lord Bootle-Cadogan they couldn't really turn her out, so with gritted teeth they had welcomed her home. For hours at a stretch she would sit under the tree reading, or thinking, or sketching a beautiful flower. Jack wasn't at all sure she'd approve of sheep and goat pellets all over its roots, although she might well have persuaded a goat to give up some milk for cheese. She was very fond of goat's cheese. In fact, she was very fond of any food that smelt of either feet or armpits . . . sometimes both . . .

Just as he was about to run after the animals and shoo them off, a dark-clothed figure stepped up from behind the tree and untied them. In the shadows of the branches it was difficult to see who it was. As Jack tried to make them out the person nodded towards the church as if paying their final respects, slid something beneath the lower rail of the fence and then led the beasts away down the hill.

'Hey, what are you . . . ?' Jack shouted, but at the same moment the chapel doors flew open and out came his father, one corner of a coffin on his broad shoulder, the opposite corner almost crippling their ancient manservant, Bone.

'Give us a hand, Jack,' hissed his father as Granny-Dazzle-in-a-crate began to list horribly to one side.

'Sorry, Pops,' said Jack, and next moment he was positioned beneath the glowing copper underside of his great-grandmother's coffin, wishing there was some way they could have avoided this, struggling behind Bone to hold everything up, hold it all together, as Granny Dazzle moved out of their lives.

3

Albert skidded backwards across the flagstones lining the tomb. The green gases were noxious, stinking, and he gagged hideously, only just managing to avoid vomiting. Hide. He had to hide. But where could one hide in a crypt only ten feet by eight, with most of the space taken up by the corpse of a grown man in a sarcophagus? There was only one option, and he really didn't like that notion.

And besides that, he had no idea what shape the spirit would take. After the initial explosion there had been no sounds other than a faint hissing, and then the thickening, the concentration of the bilious vapours along the tunnel, gathering like a storm about to break. Already they swirled in the entrance to the tomb, filling Albert with more terror than he would have thought the human body could withstand. This was beyond the familiar rapid heartbeat that indicated an exhilarating find or a new adventure. Way beyond it. Pins and needles flashed down his forearms as if he was being slashed by invisible daggers. His legs had turned to stone. The veins on either side of his neck froze into steel cords, fixing his face resolutely and unkindly on the one thing he did not want to see.

As the young man gazed upon the face appearing in the doorway, blocking his exit, he felt his eyes bulge so much that he feared they would detach themselves from his face, the pain at either side of his eyeballs screaming, ordering him to stop looking, turn away, not see.

But it was too late. The face was whole now. It was vast, repulsive and completely filling the round entrance to the tunnel. It wasn't just the entrance, Albert reminded himself — it was the exit too. The only way out. But he would never muster the courage to break through the hideous features, and, in any case, he knew that whatever was in the doorway would never let him pass. The emerald gases had deepened as they gathered, so much that now they were almost black, and the swirling, evil face of the pig opened its slavering mouth and spat out its words.

'YOU RAISED HIM.'

For a mad, fear-induced moment Albert thought it meant the man in the casket. 'No! I was trying but . . . No, my l-lord, Jay died . . . bitten . . . he's still . . .'

'Not him, fool! Osiris, the god-creature – you raised him. After my work to erase him from the earth and the afterworld.'

Albert understood instantly. The tomb he and Jay had found was said to be the final resting place of Osiris, God of Agriculture and Fertility, the green-skinned ruler who governed the afterlife. Which could only mean that this . . . this thing . . . was . . .

Seth. The God of Evil. The murderer of other gods. What could Albert do? 'My . . . lord, we did not know what we were . . . it's not too late . . .'

But the death-pig opened its mighty jaws so that Albert could see only the blood-engorged mouth as it roared: 'Too late? It is too late for you. Cursed. For-ever cursed – you and Jay, your dead master. He will serve me, help to make the undead my own. But you, weak one – you are too lowly to serve me.' The pig-eyes almost disappeared as the awful figure appraised what Albert had been doing. 'But I see that you have skills. Useful skills. Your curse will be to serve your master into eternity. Both dynasties, intertwined. Forever!'

The porcine eyes flared emerald green as the pig-spirit incanted in an ancient tongue that only Albert – and his dear dead friend – would have understood:

'In underworld, in afterlife,
Eternal torment, endless strife,
Never more to be undone
Until two true hearts beat as one.

'Die!' the monstrous pig screamed. 'Die to serve, and serve the dead.'

In that instant Albert knew something with a certainty that surpassed that of all the other discoveries he and his beloved mentor had ever made.

He was not going to get out of this alive.

He also knew, but with less certainty, that it was possible his actions had saved Lord Bootle-Cadogan. Albert crossed himself furtively below his jacket, silently praying over Jay's inert body.

The pig-face was quivering, snuffling, nosing ever closer to the coffin. Suddenly suspicion flashed across the close-set eyes and the snout puckered. 'What trickery is this? What does the scarab hide?'

Albert tried not to breathe aloud, afraid his relief might show. 'The heart,' he whispered. 'My master's heart was . . . on a string around his neck.' Tentatively he moved the golden amulet aside and picked up Diselda's locket. It didn't hold a heart, of course, only a sliver of bark and some seeds from her beloved tamarisk tree, but even at that the pig-faced god recoiled.

'Cursed!'

The face sucked back into itself. Gone? No. Gathering force. Albert shuddered, then steeled himself to finish his task. He only hoped that someone would find his clothes intact and send off the packages in his inside pocket.

A vortex, heady with poisonous fumes, swirled in the doorway, the dripping fangs and snout and flinty eyes of the pig-head swimming before him. Fine, decided Albert in a last moment of clarity. He might be forced to witness what was about to come, but Lord Jay need not. Albert reached over to his friend and closed his eyes, quickly laying on each an amulet made of faience inscribed with the black, kohl-rimmed

17

Eye of Horus. 'See you in the afterlife, my friend,' he whispered into his master's ear.

And then the vortex exploded, tossing Albert into the casket and shoving him down on to Jay's body so it was impossible to say where one ended and the other began, the handle of the scalpel sliding between Albie's ribs, the gas sucking from his brain the very essence of all his knowledge, the terrible thirst for knowledge, the rampant and unfettered curiosity that had led them here to their deaths . . .

4

Jack knew it was a weird place to hang out. He couldn't say exactly why he liked it so much, crouched among the gravestones, hearing the rats scrape by with the noises that made all the local kids – and adults – stay away. Deathly noises. Skeletal fingers scratching on granite. Corpses begging, crawling, hoping for release from their eternal resting place . . .

None of that worried Jack. He was used to being alone anyway. And he felt at home here. For years he'd helped Granny Dazzle put fresh flowers on any neglected graves, and now he felt like he was carrying on her good work. Even the stray dogs that lurked around the perimeter fence had accepted him as one of their own after a week or two of scraps and leftovers from the kitchen, and no longer snarled and spat as he approached. One of them had even become quite friendly.

'Hey, Blackie,' said Jack, patting the skinny stray on

the matted fur stretched across its skull. 'Just me again, coming to see Granny Dazzle.'

'Blackie' gazed balefully at Jack with watery yellow eyes, then trotted beside him as the boy made his way over to the family crypt. Cold nibbled at Jack's ears as he stepped, giraffe-like, over the tops of the tumble-down gravestones, making sure not to step on any newly dug graves out of respect for the dead people who had been delivered only recently to their last ever home.

'You stay out here, Blackie. Go on – go with your friends.'

The dog wagged its tail hopefully, then realized Jack meant business and slunk back into the shadows. Jack pulled a large brass key from his pocket and used it to open the crypt door. The hinges wailed mournfully as the heavy oak swung aside, as though crying for the people contained within the crypt's belly. Even that eerie thought didn't bother Jack much, however. There was nothing to fear inside the tomb. Only old friends and family.

'Great-Grandpa, hi. Hello, Great-Great-Great-Aunt Meredith. Hi, all you other long-dead rellies.'

The crypt was the size of a large bedroom, housing

a few generations of Bootle-Cadogan ancestors in pots that lined the yellow walls from floor to ceiling. Each pot sat inside a niche carved into the wall, flanked by a pair of twinkling night lights that were carefully and lovingly lit each night by Bone, who looked rather like a creature of the night himself. Now the flickering lights cast long shadows across the walls, for all the world as if fingers were reaching out of the containers of dust, of human remains, trying to get a purchase on the wall so they could release themselves from their ceramic prisons. Jack noticed the shadowy hands and waved back cheerily.

There was only one vast memorial coffin in the room, centrally located so that it dominated the stone flooring. 'Hello, Granny Dazzle. It's me, Jack. Mind if I sit on you?'

Jack stepped on the stone rim running around the bottom of the tomb then spat on his handkerchief. He cleaned off the gold plaque:

BELOW LIES LADY DISELDA BOOTLE-CADOGAN,
WHO DIED AGED 103; BELOVED WIFE OF THE LATE LORD
JACK 'JAY' BOOTLE-CADOGAN, AND ADORED MOTHER OF
LORD JACKSON BOOTLE-CADOGAN. RIP.

'When I'm Lord Bootle-Cadogan, I'll get this plaque engraved again,' said Jack solemnly, polishing up the last bit of gold. He clambered on to the tomb. '"Amazing great-grandmother of Jack Bootle-Cadogan: Granny Dazzle. When she died, a star went out in the sky". That's what I'll say.'

Jack stretched himself out to his full impressive length along the top of the coffin and pulled an apple out of his pocket. It was a good job she had been tall, towering over most men of her acquaintance apart from her husband, with her long, slender dancer's legs and high, ornate headpieces. It meant that now Jack could lie down without his feet dangling over the edge of the casing around her coffin, or his head swinging down towards the unforgiving stone flooring.

'Hmm. Comfy. I'm glad you refused to be cremated, Granny Dazzle.' Jack took a large crisp chunk out of his apple. 'So, anyway, nothing much happened today; Father was cutting the ribbon at the official opening of an art gallery somewhere in the city because they're selling off some of the family portraits – not yours, of course. Then Mother went to visit one of the kitchen staff who's just had a baby. I begged them to let me cycle to school like the other kids, but Mother insisted that Bone take me in the Daimler. It had just been cleaned and everything. Couldn't have been shinier and newer and expensiver. Might as well have had a big sign on my head: "I'M A GREAT BIG SNOBBY GIT. KICK ME."'

Jack sighed at the memory. The other schoolchildren had stared at him in disgust as he emerged from the regal car like a prince on a walkabout. He had fought a huge battle with his parents to be allowed to attend the local comprehensive, instead of prep school followed by Eton (where Bootle-Cadogans had gone since time immemorial), and he was proud of his steadfast refusal to give way no matter what bribes were offered him. Bigger horses, hang-gliding lessons, trips to Egypt and Syria to see where his great-grandfather had travelled – all had been rejected as he clung firmly to his decision to 'slum it'. But that had been just one fight, one incident in the overall campaign. It was clear that the war – the war to be 'normal' – had only just begun.

'Anyway, I managed not to get beaten up, because Bone was standing there, looking like, well, a bone actually, all white and gleaming and so old he has to be almost actually dead. But I think there'll be trouble tomorrow. Good job I stuck at it with those karate lessons, like you told me to, Granny.' Jack held the apple core up in the candle light and inspected it. He had eaten it in his particular way, his straight white teeth gnawing in different directions so the surface of the core looked like a chess-board of tiny ploughed fields. 'Anyway, I wanted to read you this.'

From another pocket, Jack pulled out a letter on thick yellow paper. 'This is really weird. I found it scrumpled up under all those bouquets you got.'

He'd been very moved by all the messages and flowers that his beloved great-grandmother had received. Long into the evenings he had sat browsing through the testimonials – 'A lovelier lady there never was', 'Thank you for the school books you donated all our lives. You got me educated proper' and 'Why were you never mine, darling D.? Mourning forever.' And then he'd come across the tattered note, not attached to any wreath, and suddenly he recalled the person with the sheep and the goats on the day of Granny Dazzle's funeral.

'It's a letter from the undertakers. I think Wee Willie Winkie must have gone mad.'

To whom it may concern,

I, Will Waite, thank you for your payment for the funeral arrangements and coffin for Lady Diselda. We receive with thanks the full terms of our agreement, namely that in lieu of 25 whole debens, we accept:

2 sycamore logs
8 sheets of copper
2 goats and
1 sheep.

It has been our pleasure to assist the Bootle-Cadogan family this past century, and we will naturally hope to continue our alliance into the future.

Yours sincerely, etc.,

William Waite
William Waite Esq.

Jack knocked on the top of the stone sarcophagus. 'Do you hear that, Granny Dazzle? You're worth half a wood pile and a couple of farm animals. I mean, I can see how logs and the copper might have been useful in making coffins – now I think about it, there was a coppery sort of finish on the bottom of your coffin – but sheep and goats? Weird. And what the bejeepers is a . . . deben?'

'It'ssssssss . . .'

Jack sat up quickly, his dark curls grazing the low roof of the crypt. 'Did . . . you say something?'

There it was again, hissing, spitting, like a low voice, somewhere close by. To his relief it wasn't coming from inside the crypt, but from outside among the gravestones. Jack exhaled quickly, hardly even aware that he'd been holding his breath. Jumping down softly from the coffin, he crept over to the door. He'd been careful to bring the key inside with him, so he was in no danger of being locked in from the outside. He hadn't, however, remembered to lock the door behind him on his way in. One push and whoever was out there could have him trapped. 'Professor Jack Plum, with the candlestick, cornered in the crypt,' whispered Jack. They had played so many board games together over the years. Granny Dazzle would have laughed at his little Cluedo joke. But there was nobody laughing now . . .

The door stood between Jack and freedom. He levered the groaning oak open a millimetre at a time. The crypt was set down a flight of steps so, even at his lofty height, Jack's eyes were only just on a level with the tips of the grave stones which leaned towards each other, whispering, telling jokes, spilling secrets . . .

Suddenly a pair of yellow eyes popped up from behind the headstone of PERCY MULLINGER, HEAD GARDENER AND DEVOTED HUSBAND. Jack gasped, but before the air had left his chest the eyes had disappeared. Blinking, Jack forced himself to calm down. It was just Blackie.

But no. There they were again – yellow eyes, but definitely human . . . ish.

Then, from behind the grave of VERA CORN-THWAITE, BELOVED WIFE, MOTHER, B-C CHAPEL ORGANIST, the yellow eyes were joined by another, even more unusual pair – bright blue irises that contrasted sharply with the whites.

For the first time that evening Jack started to feel a little worried. The worry increased when the yellow eyes turned to the sharp blue ones, and the low voice Jack had heard from inside the crypt hissed across the graveyard.

'Regard, Ice. It is him.'

'Him it is, Ozzy.' The blue eyes flicked back to Jack.

'Come along then.'

And as two unusual sets of eyes hovered before him, then raced up to meet him like four tiny space-ships, Jack forgot every karate move he'd ever learned and fell to the cold stone flags in a dead faint.

5

Jack had been moved to the top of Granny Dazzle's tomb. He came to with the feeling that he was on an operating table, with someone about to shout 'Clear!' and electrocute his chest at any moment. When nothing happened, after a few seconds, he dared to prop himself up on one elbow and look at his captors.

The golden eyes belonged to a boy, coffee-skinned and scruffy. He watched Jack intently as he sat upright, then glanced across at his companion with a slight smile on his face, as if he was watching a magic act and thinking, 'Wait for it . . . wait for it . . .' On Jack's other side, the owner of the blue eyes hopped in agitation from one foot to the other. She was better groomed than the boy, with waist-length black hair that swung in a fat plait down her spine. The blue eyes grew wider as Jack turned to look directly at her.

Jack coughed politely. 'Erm, if you're going to kill me or something, would you mind not doing it on my great-grandmother's tomb? I know she's already dead and what have you, but I'm still sure it's something she'd rather not have going on over her head.'

The boy and girl shook their heads ferociously. The boy spoke. 'We are not going to kill you. You might kill us.'

'No, no, I promise not to kill you,' said Jack. Never in a million years would he be able to kill anyone. Up at the Hall he even carried spiders outside, safely cushioned on a little hammock made of a monogrammed handkerchief. 'But . . . I heard you saying, "It's him,"' outside, as if you know who I am. Have we met before and I've forgotten? It's quite likely. Brain like a sieve,' he added cheerfully.

'Some yes and some no,' said the girl mysteriously. She reached into a fold of cloth in the long, flowing dress she wore, and pulled out a piece of paper. 'But this is you, we think.'

It was a photograph from a newspaper. On a quiet Thursday Granny Dazzle's funeral had made the headlines: 'DISELDA THE DANCING DARLING DIES', followed by a long but fairly accurate description of how Diselda Carruthers, who had outraged her well-to-do family by running away to join a dance troupe at the age of sixteen, had married a famous and noble explorer when she was eighteen, was quickly widowed and had gone on to lead an exemplary life as Lady Bootle-Cadogan. Only Jack knew that she still occasionally went out to nightclubs, heavily disguised, even after she'd turned a hundred.

'You this is?' said the boy, pointing to the image of Jack as he walked in the funeral cortège with his mother, father, various relatives from both the Bootle-Cadogan and the Carruthers sides and of course the ever faithful Bone, looking as if he belonged in the coffin rather than behind it.

'Yes, that's me. That was Granny Dazzle's funeral last week.'

The pair held each other's gaze for a moment, before the girl nodded, almost imperceptibly. 'So the lady entombed within this stone edifice – that is Diselda Carruthers who became the Bootle-Cadogan?'

Even with her foreign accent she knew to pronounce it 'Kaduggan'. So many people didn't. Jack was starting to feel slightly on the back foot. What were these people doing, circling like vultures and staring at him with their strange eyes, right in his own family crypt? Maybe he would need to use those karate skills after

31

all. 'Look, I hope you don't think I'm rude or anything, but do you mind telling me who the heck you are? And what you're planning to do with me?'

They stared at him, the girl chewing her lip, and Jack suddenly understood. 'Oh, I get it. You think I'm rich or something. Well, I might be one day when I'm Lord Bootle-Cadogan, although the estate costs a fortune to run. But at the moment I don't even get pocket money, so I can't give you any dosh, if that's what you're after. I could probably find you a spare Gameboy or two though,' he added helpfully. 'Hey, what are you . . . ?'

To Jack's astonishment, the two children had paired up at one end of the crypt, near the little altar where the vicar had made some speech about Granny Dazzle resting in pieces. Both had dropped to one knee and bowed their heads, and from beneath the tousled head of the boy came a low voice.

'Lord Jack of the dog-power, forgive our audacity.'

The girl chipped in. 'Us forgive, we implore you. You do not know us, and yet we demand of you. You know not your strength, and yet we who do know offend you. We beg your forgiveness.'

The boy lifted his head quickly, and opened his tatty shirt to reveal a bony chest. 'Or smite us now where we lie at your feet! It may indeed improve our fate now the Dazzle dies and the Seth renews and his evil rains down on our families—'

'Wha . . . stop! Stop it! I'm not going to . . . smite you. I wouldn't know how to, even if I wanted to! Just . . . Just get up, please!' Jack jumped down from the tomb and wrenched both children to their feet. 'And please don't do all that lording and begging forgiveness and stuff. I'm not a lord – not for ages, until Father dies, and I might be really ancient, like . . . thirty-five by the time that happens. And even then I just want everyone to call me Jack. Normal. Just doing nice things, like Granny Dazzle did. I know I'll be rich, but that doesn't mean I have to become a snotty prat, does it?'

The children shook their heads, a slight smile hovering at the girl's lips.

'That floor's cold, and you've not got many clothes on. Best sit on this.' Jack pulled the red velvet cloth from the altar and spread it on the ground. 'Look, tell me your names. And what you're doing here. Please.'

The children sat down obediently. 'I am Ozzy,' said the boy. 'And this is Ice.'

'Ah.' Jack had learned all about interesting names when he first went to Clearwell Comp, where some of the kids were named after characters from films and reality programme winners. 'Ozzy'n'Ice. And what do you want with me?'

'We came because of the imagery.'

'The imagery? Oh, the photograph. Right.' He didn't understand, but Granny Dazzle had taught him that a sure way to get someone to stop talking was to keep interrupting them with questions or telling them you disagreed. 'Go on.'

Ice smiled at him. 'That is all. We came because of the . . . photograph? Because the heart has stopped and the curse begins. So now it is down to you.'

'I see.' This was getting him nowhere. 'Actually, I'm sorry, I don't see at all. You came because of the photo, so you found out where we lived and came all the way here from . . . from wherever you come from, and now you want . . .'

'To live with you in all protection,' said Ozzy firmly. He crossed his arms over his chest and gave a smart nod, in a gesture that said, 'There you are, it's all very straightforward.'

'To live with me.'

Ice smiled broadly. 'We live with you. You live with us. We are – how would you say it? – yes! Family.'

'And together we find what is missing,' said Ozzy. 'My crown.'

'You've ... lost your crown?' This was getting stranger by the minute. Now the boy thought he was a prince or something.

Ozzy nodded brightly, then tipped his head forward and parted his shaggy hair. 'My crown,' he repeated, and pointed to a jagged hole in the top of his head. It was the size of a coffee cup, and Jack had to swallow hard to stop himself from vomiting on the spot.

And suddenly, as he averted his gaze politely, he understood. They were orphans, or runaways, or homeless children of some kind, and one of them needed surgery on his head. Perhaps they were escaped illegal immigrants. They certainly looked as though they came from somewhere else, somewhere hot and exotic, and their English was a little stilted. Jack's heart swelled with sympathy. Of course they were right to have come to him. He lived in a place so palatial that the bathrooms alone could have housed two whole families of refugees. They had read about this great big mansion with just one not-quite-teenager living in it and had come straight to him. For help. He would not turn them away. Granny Dazzle had taught him well.

'Right,' he said slowly, pulling on an ear lobe as he often did when deep in thought. Long floppy ear lobes ran in the family; his grandfather Johnnie, it was rumoured, had ear lobes so long he could tie them under his chin. 'So you are lost children.'

'All children are lost and found,' said Ozzy with a nod.

'Found and lost,' agreed Ice sadly.

Jack paused. 'OK. And you're brother and sister?'

Ice looked up at the ceiling in thought. 'Some yes. And some no.'

'No and some yes,' said Ozzy.

They weren't giving anything away. Jack scratched his chin. Maybe it was some sort of puzzle. 'Oh, I get it, you're twins!'

Ozzy smiled. 'Twin souls.'

'Soul twins,' said Ice, her eyes flashing briefly at Ozzy's before turning back to Jack. They were glowing so brightly that Jack was reminded of one of his skiing trips at St Moritz, when the sun reflected off the snow and seared straight through his retinas. No wonder her name was Ice.

'Your English is still a bit peculiar. Have you been learning it from Dr Seuss books? You sound like Thing

One and Thing Two in *The Cat in the Hat*. Or that wrinkled thing in the *Star Wars* films. Yoda, with the little pointy ears. Is that where you learned to speak English?' He remembered the wreath thanking Granny Dazzle for the books. 'I'll get you something a bit more advanced to read from the library. I could even do some tutoring myself. Now then,' he said, striding to the crypt door, 'let's think where I should hide you in the Hall. There are plenty of places but we'll have to avoid the cleaners, and the National Heritage ladies, who are there on open days. Come on.'

Flinging the door open, Jack turned to usher Ozzy and Ice out into the graveyard . . .

. . . only to find that they had completely disappeared.

6

What was he doing here? Who was that woman? His . . . mother? M-mother. Mumm . . . eee. He tested the words in his head, but they bounced around in the empty space like a dropped india-rubber ball. 'Mother?' he whispered, but his voice was gravelly, almost non-existent.

'Just some mail, which we dealt with,' she was whispering, the woman in the white headdress. Some kind of religious lady? No. A medical lady. A nu-nurse. 'But the rest of his clothes had to be incinerated. Covered in blood and some kind of viscous lotion, rather like amniotic fluid. His skin's raw, as if he'd been burned or exposed to acid, and around his heart is . . . Well, we've got him in here in case he scares any . . . I mean, in case the other patients disturb him.'

'All right,' said the man in the doorway, flicking over the piece of paper in his hands with a sigh.

'Good job the war's over. He couldn't have had a room to himself a few years ago. Indulgent, if you ask me.'

'But it goes with his position, doctor.'

The doctor sniffed. 'Keep me posted, matron. Don't let him move until we've established where the family is – if they're even alive.'

'Of course, doctor,' said the nurse solemnly.

Through the half-slits of his eyes, the man in the bed watched her close the door after the doctor and stick her tongue out at him. He wanted to laugh, but all that came out of his mouth was a horrific gargle, the death rattle of a drowning man . . .

The woman spun around and saw that his eyes had opened. 'Ohhh!' she said, her hands flying to her face. 'He's a-awake!' she called.

For a moment she hovered, seeming unsure whether to run after the doctor or deal with her patient. Trotting to the bedside, she looked down at him, and gave him a gentle smile. It reminded him of something. What? 'Mnggghg . . .' Mother, he tried to say. Perhaps he had just been born. That was what amniotic fluid was, wasn't it – the liquid surrounding babies in the womb. Or . . . he'd been killed. Maybe that was it. Was he dead? Alive? How to know?

He closed his eyes again as the woman ran from the room. It hurt too much to try to think. An image crept across his mind – a broad, golden expanse of water. A narrow boat, heading towards the setting sun. That's what it was like. Trying to dredge the bottom of a great river, with no idea of how deep it was, how far it would be to the other side, where it looked so inviting, or even what it was he was looking for . . .

Clothes. He suddenly remembered clothes. Incinerated, she'd said. He reached gingerly beneath the sheet and patted his arms. Ouch! Bare. Sore. He withdrew his hand quickly. Every inch of his skin was tender to the touch, and for the first time he noticed that the sheets were held above his torso on a light frame of bamboo. No wonder, as his body was streaked with blood, matted with dust, a gory red ring outlining the left-hand side of his chest. So presumably he was alive, and, wherever he was, at least they were looking after him.

As his hand pulled clear of the top of the sheet his finger caught on something rough and he cried out, his voice raw and strangulated. Pain had torched his finger, but that was nothing compared to the anguish that had ravaged him as he realized what it was that he had touched.

With exquisite care he lifted his chin so that the thing around his neck swung free, hanging down to one side of his throat. An ornate golden locket dangled from a chain, and he remembered something. Someone.

And with the sudden recollection came an immense longing.

Home.

He had to get home.

And wherever that was, it wasn't here, with the date palms flapping gently outside the window. Home was green, and hilly, and someone waited there. Waited for him. For . . . J.?

With every nerve crying out in pain, he pushed the bamboo cage off the bed. Then he levered his naked legs over the edge of the bed and wrapped himself in the bloodied sheets. His limbs were stiff. He hadn't used them for so long. How they hurt.

But the agony that would befall him if he did not fulfil his destiny would be far more painful. He had to go. Now. Shoving one sheet-shrouded foot in front of the other, trying not to groan with every step, ignoring the young nurse who saw him from the other end of the corridor and appeared to be so shocked she couldn't even scream, he stole out into the darkness.

7

'Ozzy? Ice?'

Jack's voice came out in rather a hoarse squeak. He ran quickly round Granny Dazzle's tomb to see if they were hiding. 'Come on, you two. This isn't funny. Where did you get to?'

A faint trickle of fear whispered across the back of his neck. He had been coming here, off and on, for years, with not so much as a single worry about ghosts and ghouls. For the last week, he'd been down here every night, picnicking on Granny Dazzle's tomb and having long if rather one-sided chats with her, and with Great-Grandpa Jay and any of the other ancestors whose funeral urn happened to catch his eye. But when two strange flesh-and-blood children with hypnotic, luminous eyes vanished completely from a small room with only one exit, Jack thought he might have reason to be a little afraid.

The goose pimples on the nape of Jack's neck stood

to attention again. Yes, he was definitely worried. But also . . . cold? Jack lifted a hand to his neck, and instantly felt the breath of cold air on the back of his wrist. A draught. But it wasn't coming from the doorway – was there another entrance he didn't know about? Or, more accurately, an exit?

The children had been sitting on the cloth in front of the little stone altar. Jack ran over to it. Sure enough, the cloth was no longer lying flat on the floor. Instead it snaked out from under the stone altar table, with the far end disappearing between the legs.

Jack dropped to his knees and wriggled under the altar. 'Steps! Oh my life, and a . . . a tunnel.'

This was very exciting. Now that he considered it (which he did while shuffling back into the crypt and filling his blazer pocket with night-light candles from the store in one of the niches, and grabbing a lit candle from next to his great-great-great-grandfather's pot) a tunnel made perfect sense. The Hall was a good fifteen minutes' walk from the cemetery and its tiny church – twenty or more for people with shorter legs than the Bootle-Cadogans – and Jack knew how lazy and secretive some of his ancestors had been. It was perfectly natural that they would have a tunnel leading from the Hall to the graveyard, so they could do all their weeping and wailing over dead husbands and so on without having to go outside and get wet.

'Ozzy'n'Ice! Ice'n'Ozzy!' The way they spoke was obviously catching. Jack slithered down the stone steps. When he cautiously stood upright and didn't crack his head on the ceiling, he knew for sure that the tunnel had been built by one of his ancestors, to accommodate their unusual height. 'Look, don't be frightened. I've got some candles, and this tunnel will just lead to somewhere in the Hall, so nothing to worry about. We'll have you out in two shakes of a dog's tail. Ozzy? Ice?'

There was no sign of them, so Jack trudged along the tunnel. The earthen floor was very even, with a level, soft base of fine, sandy dirt and smooth walls lined with large yellowy bricks. Someone must have had their servants working pretty hard to set all this up. And it was just as Jack had suspected: within three minutes he was climbing another set of stairs and walking through a heavy door which Ozzy and Ice had left open. Rather than looping up and down the lanes at the edge of the village, between Lowmount Hall and its graveyard, the tunnel had led him directly under the fields and presumably one or two of the estate houses in which the servants lived.

'Now where am I?' Jack felt around on the wall for a light switch. 'And where are you?'

Ozzy's voice sounded hollow. 'We sit here in the dark.'

'In the dark we sit,' agreed Ice.

Still fumbling for the electricity, Jack lifted the candle, and two pairs of eyes glimmered back at him. 'Oh yes, there you are. Like I said, nothing to be worried about. I'll just get the lights on and . . . Oh!'

If Jack had been forced to guess which room he would pop out into, he would probably have said somewhere in the east wing, the oldest part of the house. One of its bedrooms even had a minstrels' gallery, and another was completely dominated by an enormous fireplace that could have accommodated a double bed. It seemed fitting for ancestral grieving widows tunnelling to their loved one's side.

But no. They were actually in the museum. It was not a big museum, but then most people's homes, Jack assumed, did not have even a minuscule museum.

Sometimes he had to admit that there were certain advantages to being a lord-in-the-making. The Hall boasted thirty-seven bedrooms – Jack's whole class could have had one each and there would still be enough left over for the teacher, the headmaster and Jack's parents; it had a banquet hall, a ballroom (for dancing – not playing football, much to Jack's disappointment), a home cinema, various other rooms that Jack had never even investigated and an indoor swimming pool (empty), an outdoor swimming pool (green and slimy and filled with ornamental carp) and a rooftop swimming pool (also empty). Some parts were very neglected, as the Hall cost a fortune to heat and only the living accommodation and those bits that were open to the public at weekends and on bank holidays were cleaned and warmed regularly, but even the chilly bits made for a brilliantly exciting place to live and explore.

'Wow!' said Jack softly. 'I'd forgotten this was here. I think Granny Dazzle set it up. It's full of all the stuff Great-Grandpa Jay and his colleagues collected on their explorations. Look.'

The trio moved slowly round the dusty room, peering into grimy glass cases and blowing dust off the statuettes and sculptures that languished on stone pedestals. The museum was one of the uncleaned parts of the Hall, and its exhibits were quite hard to identify, but Jack pointed out the things he could remember being shown when he was very small: the theatre ticket to see a dance troupe that his great-grandfather had bought on the night he fell in love with Diselda the Dancing Darling; a collection of her costumes; guns and sabres from some terrible war; a white and shiny skull sitting atop a ragged pile of bloodied bandages.

'When I'm in charge, I'll get this place cleaned up.'

'We will clean.' Ice touched his arm lightly, and Jack suddenly felt another shiver run across his skin.

'Yes,' said Ozzy. 'Clean we will.'

'Clean you won't,' said Jack shortly. 'I mean, no, you don't need to do that. You're not my servants, you're my . . . well, my new and rather weird friends, I suppose. And you could end up with dust in your head wound, Ozzy. But you can hang out here – look, there are even a couple of beds.' He pointed to a pair of dusty camp beds pushed into a corner – an exhibit, according to the little card placed on top of one of them, from Lord Jay's voyage to the Sahara. 'I'll go and get you some food, and blankets, and what else? Water, I suppose. And I'll bring some paper so we can work out where you've come from and find your family for you. And a doctor.'

Ice and Ozzy had sat down on the camp beds, their hands folded simply into their laps and those strange liquid eyes fixed on Jack. At the mention of family, however, they lifted their hands to their faces and started to wail, rocking back and forth.

'Nooooo! No family. You are family. This is hoooooome,' cried Ice, swaying and waving her arms around like a tree in a storm.

Ozzy howled even more loudly than Ice. 'We stay. We serrrrrrrve!'

Jack clapped his hands to his ears. 'Fine, fine! Just . . . shush! Look, you can stay here for a few days – of course you can. And maybe I can . . . I don't know, persuade Mother and Father to adopt you. It's not like we haven't got enough space. But they're very funny about things like manners and proper introductions and people looking exactly right, so we'll have to get you all cleaned up first. And I won't tell them you've been living in the museum!' In fact, Jack realized, it would be wise not to mention them at all until the children were at least dressed normally.

The wailing had stopped, much to his relief. 'Good.

That's better. Now, you just sit here while I go and have a snoop in the kitchen. See if Cookie's left anything nice from dinner – she should have done; we had some Secretary of State visiting. Don't make a sound. And don't move from here.'

Ice and Ozzy nodded solemnly and were as good as their word. When Jack returned ten minutes later, bearing lamb shanks, parsnip puree, half of a very fancy apple crumble and a couple of sleeping bags, they were still sitting cross-legged on top of the dusty blankets – like Peter Pan and Tinkerbell, thought Jack, only without the fairy outfits and rather more grubby. In the half-light Ozzy looked distinctly green-tinged.

'I'll get you to a shower in the morning, so you can scrub up a bit. And I'll find you some clothes,' he said, doling out food on to a couple of museum plates marking the wedding of Prince Charles and Princess Diana. Granny Dazzle had always really loved the Royal Family. 'I'd better get to bed myself. Just let me close this door.'

The door to the tunnel was still wide open, between the tall glass cupboard containing several of Granny Dazzle's dance outfits, and something inscribed on the wall – a big dark triangle, like the tail of a fish. Jack slammed the door shut; as he did so he heard Ice and Ozzy drop to the floor once more. He didn't look round – frankly all the bowing and vowing was getting a bit tedious – but peered instead at the back of the door he had just closed. The rest of the fish, a circle within an oval, was burnt into the heavy oak, as if someone had traced out the shape with a flaming ember.

Jack stood back. It wasn't a fish at all, he could see now. It was something he'd seen rather too much of recently: a vast, luminous, golden eye.

Looking straight at him.

'Don't be ridiculous, B-C,' said Jack to himself. He had seen enough old portraits to know that the eyes always seemed to look at you, follow you around the room. It was just an artist's trick. The same was true of this eye. When Jack moved back, it gazed at him by his great-grandmother's clothes in the glass cupboard. He ran to the other side. From there it looked as though the eye was staring at the display of some very boring kitchen things, including a sieve and a set of old-fashioned scales. Further back, it just appeared flat, and once more quite fish-like. Thankfully.

Jack cleared his throat. 'That's enough for one night.'

He was suddenly very tired and quite glad when the twins lay down on their camp beds, wriggling under the sleeping bags. He laughed. It seemed there was an awful lot he would have to teach them.

Tomorrow he'd tell them that they were meant to get *inside*.

8

He could smell something different in the air, and for a moment he paused, head raised, tilting his nostrils towards the scent. Along with his swollen eyes and his blistered lips, they were the only exposed parts of his face. Saline. It was the same smell as the devastatingly painful tears that had seeped from his eyes earlier, only a million times magnified. The scent of a lifetime's tears.

It spurred him on. 'Home . . .' he tried to call out, enervated, stumbling after the smell like a hound after a fox. That's right. The hunt. Wherever home was, they hunted there . . . 'Ho-ome!' he shouted again, dragging one stiffened leg around in a loop then forcing the other ahead of it, making little headway but inching closer, ever closer, to that distinctive scent.

When the smell became accompanied by noises – lapping water, groaning machinery, the laughter and shouts and remonstrations of men – he knew that he was far enough away from the hospital to escape. The . . . the sea. That was it. The smell was the sea. And suddenly his head was filled with that same vision of a low punt, sliding over golden waters to the peace and serenity of the far bank.

A boat.

He had to get a boat to go home.

Energized, he lurched onward, bellowing as he went, as loudly as his bandaged jaw and acid-burned skin would allow. 'Home! Home!' Someone would help him. People always helped an English gentleman.

The thought made him shout with pleasure. That was it! English! He was an Englishman, so he had to get a boat back to . . . Englishland. No. Too long. To . . . Engle. Englishmanton . . . He sighed. It was far too difficult. Surely someone would be able to help him.

And suddenly he spotted that someone. Just ahead, a young man sat on an upturned rowing boat, whittling a stick into a little figurine. A *shabti*. The tiny statuettes that the ancients put in the coffins of their loved ones, so that when they reached the afterlife they'd have someone to do the work for them. *Shabti*. He tried to say the word, but his lips wouldn't meet properly, and the sound just came out as two sharp, cawing breaths.

The whittling boy glanced up from his carving at the sound, and the man staggered forward, overjoyed, his outstretched arm proffering the locket as some kind of evidence of where he came from, his head thrown back so that his blood-filmed eyes could meet the other's, his bandaged face parting at the lips as he tried to shout out – 'Home . . . Home!'

The young man stared at him, frozen, for a full half-minute. Then, to the bandaged man's great bewilderment and grief, the boy let out a blood-curdling scream that would probably have been heard back at the hospital. Scrambling backwards over the hull of the boat, the lad stuck out his whittling knife in such a frenzy that he even managed to slice through his own knee, jabbering madly in a dialect too thick and fast for the other man to follow. Trying to calm the boy down, he toppled after him, rolling from one side to the other to avoid the boat, to stop his sheet-covered skin coming into contact with the splintering, bark-rough shell of the hull, while all the time the young man shrieked and wailed and brandished the knife in his face.

And suddenly there were more of them, summoned by the young man's screams. The injured man turned to them hopefully, his arms open and welcoming, his head rolling from side to side as he tried to make eye contact from between the slipping bandages. 'Home?' he gargled hopefully.

To his horror, they gazed at him with the same fearful expression as the lad, clutching at each other's arms, silenced momentarily by the mere sight of him – of HIM, an ENGLISHMAN, for goodness sake, until suddenly all hell let loose. Grabbing whatever tools were to hand – oars, packing crates, urns filled with olives – they descended upon him as one, bellowing in fear and anger, the whites of their eyes flashing . . .

They wanted to tear him apart, limb from pustule-covered limb. Why? he wanted to ask them. What had he done to deserve this brutal attack when all he wanted was to get home? Damn it! He would demand their help. 'Home!' he roared. But the word erupted from his lacerated throat like the scream of a cornered fox, shocking even the man himself with its ferocity.

For a second, it stopped the baying angry crowd in their tracks, but it didn't help. Even hampered by his wrappings, the man could see that they weren't going to help him. In fact, they were still intending to kill him.

With one tremendous effort he picked up the edge of the overturned boat and flung it in the way of the marauding men. Then, wincing and whimpering with every step, he staggered off to one side and stumbled in a half-crouch, arms extended, legs spread apart to protect his chafed skin, to the piles of crates further along the dockside.

The men seemed in no hurry to chase after him, and after a few moments he allowed himself to slow down and then eventually to stop. He didn't want to stop. Stopping allowed the pain in. And, sure enough, as soon as he drew to a halt behind a large crate that smelt strongly of sulphur, a surging flame of agony spread from his toes to the tip of his skull. He threw back his head, trying to drag in air, and suddenly spotted the label on the side of the crate. Southampton, England.

ENGLAND! He smacked the crate in excitement, regretting it immediately as pain coursed up his arm.

Then he gasped. The crate had fallen open. Inside looked cool and dark, a respite from the sweltering heat of the surrounding air.

This crate was going to England.

Exhausted, the man crawled inside the vast wooden box, stretched out on his right side, the less painful side, and instantly fell into the brain-dead sleep of the severely infected.

9

'No, Jack, you cannot stay home today.'

'But, Mother, you HATE me going to Clearwell Comp,' Jack shouted along the length of the breakfast table. He was desperate to spend the day with Ozzy and Ice. 'What about if I promise to think about . . . you know . . . prep school?'

Bone, shuffling platters of eggs in the background, raised a scrappy eyebrow, watching Lady Bootle-Cadogan with interest from behind his tinted glasses. She pushed away her dish of mango and wiped her mouth delicately.

'Darling, you argued with us for nearly three months about your ardent and constant desire to attend that asylum you call a school. While Granny Diselda was alive we were – well, I wouldn't call it happy exactly – we were resigned to letting you give it a try. But soon you'll be thirteen. More responsibilities will soon be heading your way. You should be off to Eton soon.' His mother stood up and brushed non-existent crumbs from her skirt. 'So I suggest you get in the Daimler and go off to jolly old Clearwell. Before I change my mind and pack you off to boarding school right now, whether you like it or not.'

Eton? Boarding school! The whole thing was preposterous. He'd have to really prove himself at Clearwell. Then surely – surely – they wouldn't make him go elsewhere. Jack propped his head on his hands, miserable. 'All right. I'll go today. But please can I take my bike?'

'No. It's still dark this morning. You might hit a pothole, fall off and permanently damage your spinal column. Then not only will we have to feed you soup through a drip for the rest of your life, but also you'll never be able to play rugby when we finally get you to Eton.'

'And we can do without the expense,' chimed in Jack's father. 'Have you seen this gas bill, darling? Sixty thousand pounds! And that's just for half a year! How in the name of your prized chrysanthemums are we meant to pay that?'

Lord Bootle-Cadogan shook the bill at his wife, but Jack's mother just kissed the top of her son's head as she swept from the room. 'Bone, do you mind taking Jack to school? I've got Advanced Flower Arrangement in the lower greenhouses.'

'Ma'am,' said Bone, inclining his gleaming pate so far that Jack worried his neck might break.

Jack sighed. 'It's the Daimler again then, Bone.'

'Sir.' 'Sir' and 'Ma'am' were about the only words Bone ever uttered, dropping his jaw in an odd, clunky movement before spitting them out. But he accompanied his short words with such an array of head bobs and weaving that it was always pretty clear what he meant. This 'Sir' meant 'Sorry, buddy, but yes it's the Daimler, and nothing you or I say will get your mother to change her mind.'

'Can we at least drive it through some fields or something, so it's not quite so disgustingly SHINY?'

Bone's other eyebrow quivered and his lips straightened in a semblance of a smile. 'Sir,' he agreed.

'Tell you what, Bone – I'll meet you at the graveyard gate in twenty minutes. I want to talk to Granny Dazzle.'

The manservant simply looked at him quizzically, nodded slowly in a none-of-my-business sort of way, and left the room with a tower of serving dishes

61

between his hands like a huge cartoon club sandwich.

As soon as Bone had gone, and Jack's father was safely hidden behind his newspaper again, Jack grabbed a silver platter and swept as many leftovers as he could find on to it. For once, he didn't really want to talk to Granny Dazzle. Taking the tunnel down to the graveyard would buy him the extra time he needed to talk to Ozzy and Ice before he had to meet Bone at the gate.

Grabbing his school bag (a carefully battered sports backpack and not the polished leather satchel he would have had to use at his parents' choice of school), Jack ran through the corridors of the Hall. 'Morning, Clare! Morning, Dot!' he shouted to the cleaners who were polishing the piano in the drawing room. There was to be a big open day on Saturday, and the whole household was gearing up for it, including his mother, who had gone into overdrive on the flower arrangements and would probably strap a passing child to a garden cane and stand it in water if it hung around for long enough.

The Long Gallery went by in a blur as Jack sprinted through, passing cleaners and handymen and all manner of National Heritage people. They were recording new taped walks around the Hall, despite threats of strikes. National Heritage didn't pay people very well and employed a lot of volunteers. Jack had read about this in the local paper, and while he felt very sorry for the poorly paid employees, he found it rather funny when the article said that properties all over the country, including Tintagel and Dover Castle, were running on 'skeleton staff'. Some of them looked old enough, that was for sure.

Skeletons. The thought spurred him on. Finally the hordes of people petered out as he neared Granny Dazzle's rooms, which led on to a rarely visited area of the Hall. Amazingly, the plate of food had remained intact, and was still wafting nice smells around as he pushed open the door and stepped, panting, into the museum.

'There you go,' he said, shoving the platter on to a nearby stuffed bison. 'Breakfast. Although I see you've got most of last night's dinner left. Gosh, you didn't even touch the apple crumble. Great!' He grabbed a spoon. 'You don't eat much, do you?' Jack loved eating, and could generally do it all day without ever feeling full. Long hollow legs, Granny Dazzle used to say.

'Our hunger is different to yours,' said Ozzy calmly, perched on top of his neatly folded sleeping bag.

Jack scooped up the last of the apple crumble. 'Well, you might not need to eat much, but you definitely need to wash.' A faint smell clung to them, of . . . something . . . Damp earth? Mould? 'I've got to go to school, but I'll be back at three thirty and then I'll show you where the bath is and everything. There's a toilet just through that little door in the corner for now.'

'Oh. We come with you.' Ice climbed gracefully off her camp bed and smiled at Jack.

'No,' said Jack. 'No can do. I'd have to explain you to Bone, and to school, and . . . no. Sorry.'

With their odd, swimming eyes the two strange children looked at each other, then nodded. 'Fine. You go,' said Ozzy. 'We see you later.'

'Later we see you,' said Ice with a smile.

'OK.' Jack heaved an inward sigh of relief. He had thought for a moment they were going to be awkward and he would find himself having to smuggle the pair of them into Clearwell. Though even that might be easier than having to explain them to Bone. 'See you later. Close this door behind me, will you?'

Along with breakfast, he'd had the forethought to

bring a torch. The little tea-light candles had worked perfectly well, but they weren't exactly practical. Jack turned it on, illuminating the gold of the glowing eye on the door, and for the first time noticed that the handle was a large black knob in the middle of the door, right in the centre of the eye. Things didn't often rattle him, but he felt a little squeamish about reaching out his hand and grabbing hold of someone's pupil. Still, it had to be done, and within seconds he was trotting back along the tunnel towards the Bootle-Cadogan family crypt.

Everything was as it had been last night. As there had recently been a funeral and there was a chance the crypt would have visitors he tidied up a bit, putting the altar cloth back on the table and squaring the stone oblong over the underground steps so that they were no longer visible. Then he opened the front door to the crypt and stepped out into the graveyard.

It was still grey and gloomy, with only the faintest wisp of light appearing over the far horizon. The Daimler was just pulling up to the gate of the graveyard. It was good timing – Bone would never know that he hadn't entered the crypt the normal way. Jack raised a hand in greeting to show he was on his way, then let out a cry of alarm as an intense shadow shot across his vision.

'What the . . . ? Blackie! It's you!'

The dog was slithering around the gravestones. As Jack tried to sidestep VERA CORNTHWAITE, BELOVED WIFE, MOTHER, B-C CHAPEL ORGANIST, Blackie put his head down and butted Jack in the knees so he was pushed back down the steps to the crypt. 'Blackie, stop!' said Jack with a laugh. 'I've got to go to school. I can't play now.'

He moved forward, but Blackie did it again. Jack paused, then tried to scoot around him. The dog hunkered down on to its front paws and bared nasty yellow teeth. 'Blackie, boy, what are you doing? It's me! It's Jack. You don't want to do that to old Jacky, do you? Come on, let me pass.'

The dog quietened, so Jack took a confident step forward. To his horror, Blackie let out a horrendous yowl and a volley of barks, then lunged at him. 'Blackie, no! Aaargh!'

The not-so-friendly hound suddenly flung his teeth into Jack's wrist, worrying his hand like a caught rabbit, pulling and shaking it and dragging Jack down the crypt's stairs. Appalled, Jack looked up into the animal's yellow eyes and noticed what he had never seen before. How could he have missed it? The dog was stark, raving mad. Probably had rabies. It was going to tear him into little chunks and divide him up among his pack of strays. It would feed him to its starving children. Then they would sick him up and eat him all over again.

'I don't deserve this, Blackie,' he moaned quietly. 'I thought you were my friend.' Then he closed his eyes and prepared, as best he could, to be horribly savaged and eaten alive.

After a moment or two Jack noticed that the pressure on his hand had disappeared. So too had the slavering sounds, and the sense of impending death. He looked up into the concerned purple eyes of his manservant, the blood vessels snaking visibly below the surface of his irises. Bone's skeletal fingers were entwined in the fur on Blackie's neck. With a firm shake, the manservant rattled the salivating dog until it made a desperate gargling sound, then flung it down the path towards the edge of the graveyard. Blackie slunk away with barely a backwards glance.

'Bone!' Jack sat up, checking himself for injuries. The only mark was a long bloody scratch down his arm, where the dog's tooth had pierced his skin. 'Thank goodness! That dog was about to kill me and eat me. Twice.'

For once Bone's expression was unfathomable. He frowned slightly with a little accompanying shrug, then extended his hand as his jaw flipped open. 'Sir.'

Jack allowed himself to be helped up, and brushed off his clothes. 'Thanks, Bone. Look, don't mention this to Mother, or she'll never let me out here again. And I'd really miss my chats with Granny Dazzle.'

At this, Bone raised both eyebrows, then swept out an arm to indicate that Jack ought to get in the car.

'Of course. Thanks, Bone. Let's go. I'll be late otherwise, and it's sports first thing. I do hope it's long-distance today.'

If there was one thing Jack was good at, other than dishing out dainty cucumber sandwiches on to doilies without laughing, it was running. This was a skill born out of necessity. To get from one end of Lowmount Hall to the other without it taking forever, he had trained himself over the years to pelt along at full tilt, taking the corners like a speed skater, occasionally slipping on the polished parquet, but always managing to beat his previous record of getting from A to B.

Unfortunately however, unless Jack knew the journey from A to B very well, he often didn't get there at all. His sense of direction was nil. The time he had been sent down to Bone's cottage to fetch him when Granny Dazzle was taken ill was a prime example. Two hours later his great-granny's paramedics had found him, cornered in a field by the local bull. Jack had no idea which way he was meant to have gone, or how he had ended up there. He'd just run, very fast, along the lane that he saw Bone disappearing down each night.

As soon as the manservant had driven away from the school gates Jack jumped in a nearby puddle to muddy his shoes and trousers, and rearranged his tie into a messy straggle. Thus prepared, he set off into Clearwell Comprehensive. His mission in life was to be treated in exactly the same way as the other kids. He'd changed his viola lessons to rock guitar. He'd mastered DS, PlayStation and swap cards in place of Chess Club and Advanced Archery, and when he got beaten up each day he deliberately avoided using his ever-so-precise karate skills to retaliate. The terrifying

Minty West had made it *her* mission to try to pummel him to a pulp whenever she saw him, and he'd become used to the fact. Life was getting into a sort of rhythm.

'Good morning, B-C,' said a voice behind him, so painfully aristocratic that the initials came out as 'Beah-Ceah'.

'Finch, don't say that.' Jack hitched up his backpack, glaring at the boy who'd just greeted him. Gouldian Finch was one of the main reasons Jack regularly got attacked. While Jack was busy trying to blend in, Finch brayed loudly about his upper-class background and close friendship with the local nobility, including the Bootle-Cadogans and the family of a celebrity decorator who lived nearby. Jack had never even heard of the Finch family before coming to Clearwell – but now he found himself having to fend the oily boy off at every turn.

'What? Beah-Ceah?' Finch peered at Jack down the length of his narrow, beaky nose.

'No, not that bit. "Good morning". Nobody says, "Good morning," apart from the headmaster. Say, "awright" and sort of wiggle your eyebrows at me. Or just, like, grunt and toss your hair about a bit.'

Gouldian Finch shook his head, hurrying after Jack

as he loped away on his long legs. 'You should be proud to be different. You know, if you don't speak the way you were raised to speak, they're never going to accept you for what you *are*, B-C.'

'See, that's where you and I are different,' said Jack, pulling out his map of the school. Bone had helped him to produce it when Jack had failed to find his way to double maths twice in a row. 'I don't want to be accepted for what I am. I want to be accepted for what I'm not.'

'Well, you'll never manage that either. Not unless you can pull off something stupendous. Something incredibly "cool",' and here Finch stopped to mime speech marks in the air. 'Win the Clearwell Comp Comp or something.'

'Fat chance of that.' Jack turned his map upside down to try to work out where he was in relation to his destination. 'I can't even find the gymnasium – I mean, sports hall. I'd better go. See you, Finch.'

'*Au revoir, mon ami*. You'd better start calling me Gouldian, by the way. Surnames are *sooooo* public school.' Finch saluted smartly and turned on his heels. 'Oh, and one small thing – you're going the wrong way. You'll end up in the kitchens. Turn right around, and take a left at the end of this building. You do know which is left?'

'Of course I do!' said Jack, smiling weakly. Actually Jack was never entirely sure, but he wasn't about to let Finch – Gouldian – know that.

By the time he arrived at the sports hall the others were already changed and heading out for basketball. He got into his shorts quickly and joined the end of the line. On the changing-room door was a poster for the Clearwell Comp Comp Finch had mentioned. It was a cross-country run, rough enough to be considered appropriate by the toughest of Clearwell's kids, and cool enough to ensure complete acceptance for anybody who won. Minty West had already signed up in crude capitals written in red pen. Or blood. Jack sighed. It would be such a joy to win it. Nobody would care about the Daimler any more. He might even avoid the beatings-up. Before he really knew what he was doing, Jack grabbed the pen on the end of its piece of string and added his name to the bottom of the list.

'Come on, Posh With Dosh!' yelled the sports teacher, Mr Guisely. Jack despised him. With Guisely constantly singling him out for attention, and with

Jack's innate good manners making it impossible to be rough when there were girls playing too, his basketball career seemed doomed to failure, despite his height advantage. 'You can mark Minty. Try and get the ball off her at least once – and not by asking politely.'

'Minty? But Minty's a . . .' Jack stopped short when he saw the look on his opponent's face.

'A what?' The girl's short dark hair swung menacingly around her solid jawline. 'A girl? I could 'ave you any day, Lord Fancypants. And I quite often do,' she added in a nasty undertone.

Jack thought quickly. 'Not "Minty's a girl". No, I'd never say that. I meant, Minty's a killer. That's what I was going to say. A killer. I know full well you could, erm, "'ave me", that's why I was wondering if Guisely could put me up against someone a bit less . . . impressive. It's going to be such a walkover for you. What a boring game you'll have!'

Minty sneered, but Jack could see that his words had sunk in. In the right light, the sneer might almost have been a satisfied smile. 'You're a bigger girl than I am,' she said softly. 'Just get on with it, will you? And don't make me hurt you.'

'No. Sure. Certainly. I'll just, you know, wave my

arms around a bit so Guisely thinks I'm doing something, but otherwise the game's all yours.'

'OK.'

The pair shimmied around each other, looking busy enough to avoid attention, with Jack darting nimbly out of the way of the occasional shove from Minty that was her own version of sport. There wasn't actually much for them to do, to Jack's relief. The basketball champion for the year, the frostily capable Fraser Adams, bobbed up and down at the other end of the court, dunking ball after ball through the opposition's hoop.

'You were right, Fancypants,' said Minty in a low voice. 'This is getting boring. Go and get the ball and fetch it down this end. Let me have a go at scoring.'

'But I can't go right the way down there,' said Jack. 'Guisely will kill me! I'm supposed to be marking you.'

'Well, I'll mark you if you don't,' said Minty with a grim smile. 'So it's your choice: Guisely or me.'

There was no competition. The worst that Guisely could do would be detention and a few lines. Minty's punishment could run to broken bones, and that was if he was lucky and didn't find himself upside down in a toilet. A girl's toilet. With a sigh, Jack turned around and trotted off down the length of the basketball court. Maybe this wouldn't be too difficult after all, especially as he was a good head taller than most of the other players. He'd just have to get the ball, then pretend to fumble it somehow so that it bounced up the other end to Minty, unmarked and positioned for victory.

Guisely hadn't noticed him yet, so Jack skirted a couple of the lazier players who were trying to look busy on the edges of the court and skidded closer to their star shooter. The ball was arching towards him, firing comet-like through the air, just about to be caught up and slammed into the hoop once more.

Jack leaped into action, bouncing on the balls of his feet and reaching out his arms to intercept the ball . . . then suddenly he froze. At each corner of his end of the basketball court stood a child with great luminous eyes, one gold pair and one icy blue.

'Nooooo!' he cried, his mouth gaping in a mighty roar as every player in the room turned to look at him, and then followed his eyes to the new pair of kids in the sports hall, the most un-normal-looking kids ever, who were obviously there with Jack Bootle-Cadogan, Lord Posh With Dosh Fancypants.

And just at that moment Jack noticed the ball was right in front of his face. Before he knew what he was doing he opened his mouth even wider, impossibly wide, and caught it between his open jaws. As his feet hit the floor again he remembered Minty's instructions, and slowly yanked the ball off the points of his teeth. He spun around, surrounded by confused and angry basketball players and one seriously upset sports teacher, and threw the whistling ball over their heads. It was going to be all right, Jack thought as he made contact with the bleached wood floor; Minty had the ball.

But suddenly the whistle blew and Guisely stomped over furiously. 'What are you doing, you freak? You burst the blasted ball! We can't play with it now.'

'I . . . what?' Jack felt a little dazed.

'And a couple of other things, while we're at it,' said Guisely, breathing cigarette fumes into Jack's face. 'Why were you throwing the ball to Minty? You do know she's on the opposing team, don't you? You were meant to be marking her, you moron. At best, I'll assume you really are that stupid and forgot what team she was on, because otherwise I'd have to imagine that you were trying to skew the game, Posh Boy. And I do not tolerate cheating!' He pulled Jack to his feet, which was not too easy since he was actually shorter than Jack and had to glare up at him. 'And one last thing, Posh,' he said, gesturing angrily at Ozzy and Ice. 'We do not allow servants or whatever they are to come and watch. This is school, not the flipping polo club.'

'They're not servants,' said Jack, horrified at the idea. Even *his* family didn't employ children! 'They're . . . well, I'm kind of adopting them until they can find a home.'

Guisely was quaking with fury, specks of saliva glistening on his lower lip. 'I'll find you a home, Posh Boy. In detention – every night this week.'

Jack brightened a little. Detention was generally considered to be quite cool, and a whole week's worth would probably ratchet up some much-needed popularity points. He nodded at Mr Guisely, trying to look ashamed.

'And just to ensure she knows that cheating will not be tolerated, if that's the little stunt she was trying to pull, I'd better send Minty along with you.' Guisely marched over to the girl and picked up the flattened

77

basketball that lay like a frisbee at her feet. 'Minty, every night, and no excuses!'

Jack caught Minty's eye, and his heart sank. In fact, it felt as though it had completely disintegrated. For a moment he wished he was back in Blackie's jaws – being gobbled up as dog chow was looking a whole lot more pleasant than whatever Minty had in mind for him. This time he was definitely dead meat.

10

To Jack's huge relief, Minty didn't turn up for detention. He sat quietly, writing his essay on 'Why cheats in ancient civilizations were stoned to death', ready for the door to fling open any moment and for Minty to strut in, furious and terrifying. Mr Guisely prowled between the windows and the door, waiting for the girl to come into view, looking more thunderous with each passing minute.

'She's in trouble. Oh yes. She's in so much trouble. Do you hear me, Posh Dosh?'

'Yes,' said Jack with a serious nod. 'Yes, I do. Trouble. Perhaps she forgot. Would you like me to find her?'

He might as well have suggested stepping into a bullring in a big red cape. Sometimes Jack wished he wasn't quite so . . . so nice. So willing to see both sides of everything. Always trying to keep all of the people happy, all of the time. Granny Dazzle had said that it was because he was a Libran, born under the sign of the scales like the ones she'd given him as a christening gift, the very ones he'd offered up for the museum. 'A born mediator,' she'd told him. Well, it wasn't helping him much now.

Guisely spun round, the heel of his trainer squealing on the wooden flooring. 'Oh. Oh yes. You'd like that, wouldn't you, Posh? Cheat your way into detention and then cheat your way out of it. "Oh, sir, I couldn't find her,"' whined the teacher in a scratchy falsetto that Jack hoped was nothing like his own voice. '"Sir, I think she's gone home. Sir, my servants are waiting for me so I've got to go." I don't think so. You'll sit right there until I say you're good and ready to go, and then you'll come back and do the whole thing all over again tomorrow night. And the next night. And, what else was it? Oh yes, two nights after that too. Got it?'

Jack practically saluted. 'Sure. Yes, of course. With pleasure, sir. I was just trying to be helpful. And, sir, by the way, hope you don't mind me mentioning it again, but they really aren't my servants.'

'But, Posh Dosh . . .' Guisely gestured to the window. 'They're outside, waiting to carry you home, by the look of it. Don't pretend you didn't know.'

At that, Jack risked extending his detention further by leaping out from behind his desk and running to the window. It was true. Ozzy and Ice were sitting at the bottom of the school steps beside a curtained contraption. Jack squinted to get a better look. Red and gold material flapped luxuriantly on top of some kind of stretcher. It looked like the kind of rig-up that ought to be on top of an elephant, transporting Indian nobility.

Guisely appeared next to him at the window. 'You couldn't just adopt a stray cat, could you, Posh Boy? No, you have to be all Lord-of-the-Manor and take in a couple of refugees and their sedan chair, or whatever it is.'

'I think it's a camp bed, sir.' As he stared Jack was able to work out what the strange pair had concocted between them. Guisely was right – it clearly was a sort of sedan chair, made up of one of the camp beds, the red velvet altar cloth from the crypt and something shiny in turquoise and gold that looked like Granny Dazzle's belly-dancing costume from the museum. And, from the looks of it, they intended to carry Jack home on it.

Guisely surveyed him with a look of utter disgust.

'Go on, get out. Sick of the sight of you. But don't think that I don't expect to see you tomorrow.'

'No, sir. Or rather, yes, sir. Same time, same place.'

'Make sure they don't drop you,' said Guisely, sounding very much as if he would love them to drop Jack, preferably in something unspeakable that would render him smelly, dirty, or perhaps even dead. 'And try having a wash before you turn up tomorrow.'

'Um . . . right.'

What was that supposed to mean? Fag-Breath Guisely was the smelly one, thought Jack as he sprinted off towards Ozzy and Ice. They stood up the moment they saw him and bowed their heads politely.

'We bear your burdens as our own and carry you to your abode,' said Ozzy in a low chant. He nodded to Ice, and in unison they lifted up the camp bed and waited for Jack to clamber aboard.

Jack was genuinely touched. 'That's really, really lovely of you, but there's absolutely no need. I'm sure Bone will be waiting for me.'

'No, we will carry!' Ice sounded quite insistent, and Jack suddenly saw a flinty resolve in her unusual blue eyes.

'Carry we will,' echoed Ozzy.

'Look, I'd love to, but . . .' Jack thought quickly. It was more than his life was worth to climb on to a decorated camp bed and be carried regally from the school premises. Even at this time, someone would be bound to see. One word to Minty, and he'd be as dead as Granny Dazzle. But he didn't want to upset his new friends, especially when it appeared that disagreeing with them made them more determined than ever. He tried another tack. 'I'll be honest with you both. If I get on this thing, word will get around the school in seconds and I'll be so beaten up you'll never recognize me again.'

Ice jiggled her end of the camp bed to get Ozzy's attention. 'You understand, Ozzy? He will be dead. Now is not the time.'

'Fine,' said Ozzy after a long pause. 'We are sorry for upset causing you. Better perhaps it is if you go with your bone.'

'Oh, Bone's a person, sort of a ser–'

Jack stopped short. There was no point his getting all offended about Guisely thinking that the strange-eyed twins were his staff. Time to get real – he *did* have servants, and Bone was one of them. The only thing was, Bone had been with them for so long that Jack

83

thought of him as a fixture of Lowmount Hall – more of a friend or an old relative than an employee. No one in the family could even remember a time when Bone hadn't been there. 'Bone always comes to collect me, and he'll worry if I'm not there,' he mumbled.

The twins nodded in unison. 'Of course. You go now,' said Ozzy.

'Now you go.' Ice smiled at him, the dark shadow in her eyes completely gone.

'Thanks, guys. I will go on the sedan chair one day, I promise. Just not here, not at school.'

His long legs carried him to the car in no time. Bone was busy daubing mud on the silver radiator grille, and the Daimler looked like an all-terrain army vehicle. Jack grinned. 'That's fantastic, Bone. It hardly looks expensive at all now. Sorry I'm late – I got detention.'

Bone simply smiled as though he approved, and opened the door for Jack to get into the passenger seat, which he preferred to the vast and empty back seat from which he had to yell to be heard. Although there were a couple of people who could have used the back seat at that particular moment . . .

'Bone, I think I've just been a complete cretin and

really rude,' said Jack, smashing his backpack beneath his feet to give it an extra battering. 'Do you think we could give a couple of . . . friends of mine a lift? They could come for tea.'

'Sir.' Spinning the wheel expertly, the leather whispering against the papery skin of his palms, Bone nudged the Daimler down the school drive. But when Jack got out of the car and looked around, the twins were nowhere to be seen. 'That's weird – never mind, they must have gone,' said Jack. The interior light glanced across his face as he settled back into his seat, and suddenly Bone sucked in a tiny whistle of air.

'Bone? What is it?' The manservant was staring at him in a way that made Jack feel quite uncomfortable.

'Sir.' Bone's voice was low and concerned, with a hint of something else that Jack couldn't identify. Slowly he turned the rear-view mirror in Jack's direction. Jack stared into it, puzzled. 'Oh! Now I see what Guisely was on about when he said I needed a wash. It's just mud, or maybe ink. Yes, ink, I'd say, in that blue-black colour. I must have been rubbing my chin while I was thinking about cheating in ancient civilizations. It'll come off.'

Jack licked the end of his finger and reached out to rub at the dark shadow covering the lower half of his face. The tip of his finger made contact with his chin, and Jack pulled it away as if it had been burned.

It wasn't dirt, or mud, or even ink.

It was stubble.

Jack Bootle-Cadogan, still a couple of months from being a teenager, was growing a beard. A serious one, by the looks of it. Jack felt sick. 'Get me home, Bone.' He slumped back in his chair, too disgusted to look at himself any more. He needed yet one more thing to make him stand out at school about as much as he needed Ozzy and Ice trying to stretcher him around the school grounds. 'Take me home, quickly please. I need to get this OFF!'

11

He awoke after a long time – maybe several days, he suspected, judging by how much more easily his eyes flew open. They were no longer gummed together with congealed blood, like sealing wax on an envelope. The slumber must in some way have been healing. But his eyes still hurt. Good lord, did they hurt!

He lay back, breathing hard, closing his eyes again. Then, bit by tentative bit, he checked over the rest of his body. Feet? A little better, now that they had been rested during his stay in the crate. Legs – not so sore to the touch, but still stiff as pokers, as if his joints had fused into a locked position. Stomach? Churning. Horribly. Eugh. But that was probably because – ah, that was right – he was on a boat. Going to . . . England.

'Home,' he whispered, but his voice still cracked like that of the very devil himself.

Water. He needed water.

As far as he could see – and that wasn't far – the

only other thing in the crate he had chosen to sleep in looked like another crate. Bracing himself against the onslaught of pain, the man levered himself up, shielding his face from the dappled daylight filtering through the gaps between the boards above. Now he could see what it was. As he couldn't even remember his own name, he was mystified at how easily the word for this contraption drifted into his mind. Portmanteau. A trunk. Portable wardrobe. Good heavens, he knew some incredibly big words. He was like a walking – well, stumbling – lexicon. So who was he? What was he? Educated, obviously. A gentleman, for sure. And an invalid. Definitely, now, an invalid. Some part of him knew that there had been a war. Perhaps he'd been injured in it – many men were, often fatally. Millions had died. But that had been years ago, in 1918. Three years? Four? He didn't know.

Foraging through a pull-out drawer of silken undergarments, noticing for a moment how gently the material stroked his flayed skin, he realized that this was a lady's wardrobe. So he was all the more amazed when he pulled out the opposite drawer and found a silver hip flask. Eagerly he tipped it up to his lips, then screamed as the liquid seared his throat.

Gin! At some point he might be glad of it, but not now, now when he just wanted to assuage his hideous thirst, put out the fire that was blazing in his gullet and further down, deep inside him.

Disgusted, he cast the flask to one side and proceeded to rifle through the rest of the things. There was nothing to drink, but he was very surprised to find a small pistol, a pair of men's spectacles and a jar of what looked like grey sand in the same drawer as the flask. He held up the glasses and had an idea. Dipping a scabby finger into the jar of dust, he smeared the grey powder across the lenses of the spectacles, first one and then the other. Then he held them in front of his face and gingerly, as painstakingly as if someone was holding a gun to his head, turned to face the dim light in the corner of the crate.

Eureka! It worked – he was protected from the brightness that might not have bothered him before, but now seemed to sear straight through his retinas. Promising himself that he would return the dusty spectacles at the right moment, he studied the hole he'd created in the side of the crate.

He gasped. One slight pull, and the whole side of the crate disintegrated into a heap of jagged splinters.

He turned back to the portmanteau thoughtfully. How to protect his feet? In one of the lower drawers there were several pairs of ladies' shoes, including a pair of bedroom slippers made of red silk. As they were, they wouldn't fit, so the man bit the toe off each shoe, and then, moaning softly as his sore legs complained about the motion, he bent over and slid his feet inside. His mutilated toes poked out, blackened and repulsive, but the soles of his feet were protected now by a layer of silk-covered kid leather as well as his home-made bandages. Feeling rather pleased with himself, the man slowly clambered up the other crates as he had once climbed the pyramid in Luxor (another fleeting memory that came to him almost as a dream), then opened the trapdoor up to the main body of the ship.

The sun had set now, and he was grateful. He staggered across to a nearby cabin, overjoyed at the prospect of getting some help. People! Lots of lovely people, dining, laughing, dressed in all manner of finery, apart from the locals, who were in simple cotton shifts as they served the gentry. The man knew instinctively that these finely dressed chaps were his sort. He was one of them. With barely a thought for his blistered hands, he rapped on the window of the cabin.

But somehow his fist didn't stop at a gentle tap. Instead it plunged straight through the glass and ripped the whole frame from its housing, so that it dangled from his bandaged arm like an outsize bracelet. The commotion caused the diners to turn around, and suddenly the room erupted. Chairs clattered to the deck as the diners leaped to their feet, pushing over the table in their hurry to back away from him, one man picking up and waving a carving knife in a way that reminded him horribly of the locals at the portside. Ladies screamed, older ladies fainted, and the serving men threw dishes at him as the diners rushed through to the salon next door . . .

They didn't understand! Oh, how he wished he could summon the right words from his ravaged mouth. He put up a hand, only to discover that the material of the red silk slippers still trailed from his lips like rivulets of blood. No wonder he couldn't speak! Spitting it out from between his cracked lips, he shook his head frantically and pounded on the remaining wall; terrified screams issued from the cabin as the wood exploded beneath his fist. 'Home! Ho-o-o-o-ome,' he cried, with as much yearning as he could muster.

Once again, the scene before him turned ugly. Why did this keep happening to him? After ushering the last of the ladies through to the salon, the men turned as one – one many-clawed beast – and fanned out across the dining room towards him, carving forks and knives and candelabra held out before them, some in the shape of the cross . . .

Then he saw the wild, fevered glint in the eye of the nearest fellow, and he recognized it. Part fear, part elation. The joy of the hunt.

And he was the prey.

Thankful once again for the red slippers, he turned on his heel and lumbered away across the deck. In searing agony he dropped straight through the open trapdoor on to the ziggurat of crates in the cargo hold, retching as he tumbled down them, shattering them with every twist as if they were made of spun sugar, and finally, finally, recognizing the crate that had been his haven for a few short days.

He wrenched open the door of the portmanteau and hid himself among the soft silken folds. Sobbing gently, he found the silver hip flask and upturned it into his mouth, swallowing the pain along with a half-pint of gin.

12

Bone was pretty handy with a cut-throat razor. Electric shavers probably hadn't been invented when the man-servant started shaving, thought Jack, whenever that was. It felt very strange, sitting in Bone's bare little cottage, spotlit by the dim naked bulb that swung from the low ceiling, and hearing the rhythmic *scrape-swishhh* as Bone removed the prickly blue-black hair from his skin.

'It can't be a proper beard,' Jack argued awkwardly, his tongue in his cheek as Bone had instructed him to do in a careful and very unfunny pantomime. 'I'm nowhere near old enough. Even if I did start to get a hairy face, it would only be a tiny bit, wouldn't it? Whatcha call it – peach fuzz on my top lip. A bit of bum-fluff. That's all, isn't it? What did you have when you were . . . oh. Sorry.'

Bone paused for a moment, tipping his own head to one side as he ran his hand thoughtfully across his upper lip. It was as smooth as glass. Too late Jack realized that part of Bone's condition – albinism, as Granny Dazzle had taught him it was called – was presumably that he didn't grow facial hair. After a moment Bone shrugged, then motioned to Jack that he should move his tongue to the other cheek.

'Maybe it's a trick,' spluttered Jack suddenly. 'Guisely did something to me in detention, I bet. Messed with my pen or something. He must have been killing himself laughing inside.'

Bone squinted at him, then held out the razor. Tiny shards of blue-black hair were scattered along its length. Definitely not ink. Jack groaned. 'What is wrong with me?' he whispered. 'Am I a . . . werewolf?'

To Jack's consternation, Bone seemed to consider the question quite carefully. He opened Jack's mouth and tapped the top of a tooth with his finger. 'Ssssiiiir,' he hissed in his strangled voice. It sounded like 'Ow!' Jack remembered the basketball incident with new understanding. He *was* a werewolf.

'Are you nearly done, Bone?' he asked, wanting to cry.

In answer, Bone dabbed at Jack's face with a heavily perfumed towel and inspected his handiwork, squinting upwards at Jack's chin. Jack was nearly blinded by the flash of light reflecting off the man's gleaming pate. Finally Bone nodded and held up a small bronze hand mirror. 'Sir.'

The face gazing back at Jack was his own once more: pale-skinned, clear-eyed and curly haired. No dark, insidious stubble marking his chin, his cheeks, his . . . his forehead. Jack smiled. Werewolf? What a ridiculous thought! He was just growing up, that was all. 'Much better. Thank you, Bone. Now, would you mind giving me a lift up to the Hall?'

Bone jangled his car keys at Jack, then opened the front door for him. As Jack walked past the hall table he glanced again at the small mirror, now lying face down. He stopped and stared at it. 'Bone, that picture on the back of your mirror – that funny fishy-eye thing – it's exactly like one I've seen in Granny Dazzle's museum.'

At the mention of her name, Bone bowed his head sadly. 'Sir.'

'Oh cripes! It was a present, wasn't it? From Granny Dazzle. I'm sorry – I shouldn't go nosing into your private things. Come on, forget I mentioned it, and let's go.'

It was strange. Jack had known Bone for his entire life, as his father had before him, and yet he knew virtually nothing about the man – where he went when he wasn't busy up at the Hall, even whether he had a family of his own. Judging by the stark and chilly interior of the cottage, Jack guessed that any family Bone might ever have had must be long gone.

Back home, Cookie had laid out his dinner at one end of the long pine kitchen table – which meant that his parents must be dining with guests again. Until recently he'd usually eaten with Granny Dazzle; now he preferred eating on his own to formal conversations with visiting lords and ladies. Jack grabbed the plate of beef Wellington and steamed vegetables, helped himself to a loaf of organic uncut white from the larder and trotted off down the corridor towards the museum. Voices were drifting out of the drawing room, so he tiptoed past, then sped up again the minute he felt he was out of earshot.

But just as he thought he'd escaped there was the scrape of a chair and his father walked out. 'Jack! Come and meet Mr Ngewieke. His son's also starting at Eton soon.'

Jack stared at his father as if he was seeing him for

the first time. Maybe he could help! They were family, for goodness sake. Shared the long ear lobes and everything. 'Actually, Pops,' he said softly, 'I'm not feeling quite . . . right. Can I talk to you about something?'

His father recoiled. 'Oh good lord! You're not getting that . . . that puberty thing, are you?'

'Er . . . maybe. Did you . . . did you grow a beard when you were really young? When you were twelve, for example?'

'Don't be ridiculous!' snapped his father, shuffling backwards towards the dining room. 'That would be unnatural.'

It certainly felt it. Perhaps . . . 'Um, Pops, you know that curse that Granny Dazzle told me about . . .'

'Absolute unmitigated tosh!' interjected his father. 'What in the name of gossiping grannies are you worrying about that for? It was just silly woman tittle-tattle. They do that, Jack. You'll learn. These women are a mystery.' He perused the corridor shiftily. 'And talking of which, if you have any other of these . . . you know . . . personal questions, might I suggest that you ask your mother. Or Bone.'

'But Bone can't speak,' said Jack.

'Quite right,' replied his father absently, already

closing the dining-room door behind him. Jack's presence was no longer required, it seemed.

Slightly subdued, Jack jogged through the dim and shadowy corridors. He nodded to a couple of ancestral paintings in the Long Gallery, then smiled at the last one in the row. 'Can't stop, you two, I've got some lost children to feed. You'd like them; they're slightly peculiar. But I'll come down to the crypt and have a chat with you later.'

Grandpa Jay and Granny Dazzle beamed down at him from the portrait. It had been painted the day after their wedding, with Granny looking exotic and doe-eyed and mysterious, and Grandpa upright and proud with a broad grin, one arm around his new bride, a huge gun under the other. Jack sighed. He wished he'd seen them like that. Wished he'd seen his great-grandfather at all . . .

He tore himself away to make it to the museum before the beef Wellington was completely cold. Ozzy and Ice might enjoy this, or he was quite happy to eat it for them if they were still on their strange 'no food' diet. He'd have to get Cookie to make something they'd like, perhaps with rice and chickpeas as they didn't look like meat-eaters. 'Don't know how you got away from school so quickly,' he shouted as he shoved open the door with his foot. 'I came back for you, but you were . . . gone.'

And now they were gone again. The camp bed had not been returned, but Jack could see that Granny Dazzle's belly-dancing silk had been placed once more on the dummy in the glass cabinet. Only one thing for it. He fished in his pocket for his little torch and headed off to the crypt.

The crypt was considerably darker than usual. 'Hello?' said Jack hoarsely. He had been in here a hundred times or more, but somehow this time it felt as though he should be quieter. He looked at the candles flickering on the altar and noticed that the altar cloth was still missing. There was no sign of the children at all, but the door was slightly ajar.

Something else felt odd too. Jack couldn't put his finger on what it was. It came to him when he moved across to get up on to Granny Dazzle's tomb. The candles. There weren't normally any night lights on top of the granite sarcophagus. He climbed up anyway, carefully, but instead of lying down as usual he stood at one end of the stone slab, his dark curls almost brushing the ceiling, and studied the candles. They were in a pattern, he realized. A familiar shape. 'It's that eye thing again!' It was the same fish-shaped eye that covered the doorway from the museum, and that had adorned the bronzed hand mirror at Bone's house. An Egyptian eye, he realized suddenly, and of course that would make sense, given Grandpa Jay's interest in all things Egyptian. He thought he remembered Granny Dazzle saying once that it was the Eye of Horse, or something. He'd have to look it up.

Jack smiled. 'You should see this, Granny. Bone has done that eye shape you're so fond of, all in candles. It's like a big granite birthday cake.'

Something stopped him in his tracks. The flames of the candles guttered; Jack turned around to see if either door had opened. 'Hello? Bone? Ozzy'n'Ice?' There was nobody there.

He turned back to the candles, and suddenly Jack realized that there *was* somebody there. Except that some*body* seemed to be the wrong word, as the person standing in front of him on the tomb was quite clearly *without* a body . . . was made, in fact, entirely out of candle smoke.

'Granny Dazzle!'

Jack staggered backwards and crashed to the floor as the ghostly figure raised her arms. There was his great-grandmother, exactly the same size and shape and appearance as she'd been a couple of weeks ago before she died, but somehow cobwebby and see-through, with odd wisps of candle-smoke feathering the top of her head, and flames licking around her ankles.

'Granny . . . Granny Dazzle,' whispered Jack again. 'Is that you, or are Ozzy'n'Ice playing games with me?'

But the wispy figure of his great-grandmother was spreading her hands towards him and shaking her head.

'No? So it's really you?'

She flickered and faded a little, but Jack could see she was opening her mouth. 'What? Can you speak? What do you want to say?'

And though Jack couldn't hear a thing he could see her lips move, forming a single word. 'Museum? Yes, I know. I was in there just before. It's fabulous.'

She shook her head again, mouthing the word 'museum' over and over, faster and faster. The flames were rising and flickering from the candles up her legs, until they engulfed her, blending with the smoky form until all Jack could see was fire . . . then, with a *phhhht*, the candles went out.

'Granny! Come back! What do you mean?' Jack sat up, rubbing his head, which had bounced rather too hard off the flagstones. Maybe the candles were giving off some strange hypnotic gas. Had he been hallucinating?

But somehow Jack knew that he hadn't. He ran back to the museum, wondering if she might pop up again there. Perhaps she was playing some kind of dead treasure hunt with him, mentioning the room that would house the next clue.

But she wasn't there. Nobody was there, apart from the odd shrunken pygmy head and the stuffed bison.

It was all rather irritating, Jack felt. If he wasn't doing impersonations of Blue-Beard, or having strange gooey-eyed kids follow him round school, he was seeing his dead great-grandmother mouthing words at him before going up in smoke.

It was all a bit much, he thought, when all he'd ever wanted was to be normal.

13

Creaking. Groaning. And for the first time in a long while, it wasn't coming from him.

The man sat up carefully, his head throbbing from the combination of the residual pain in the whole of his body, and the thick musky honey wine that had been the only thing that had stood between him and certain death from dehydration. Ropes and pulleys were making the noise directly over his head. The ship had docked, and now the crates were being removed one by one from the hold. Any moment now, the tackle would swing across to his crate and he would be discovered. And no doubt chased once more by marauding strangers.

Shuddering, the man stared down at his legs. He had managed to find fresh sheets in one of the cartons, and box upon box of raw, downy cotton with which to replace his bandages and padding each night. Apart from the blood-crusted outline on the left of his chest that he was unable to wash off, his skin felt much improved – although every time he changed the dressing he was shocked at how his wound gleamed in the shafts of moonlight, repellently pale and shiny, like snake skin.

What now? If they found him encased from head to toe in stolen sheets, they would think him a vagrant. He would be thrown into prison, or some such, and he would never get home.

There was nothing for it. Sighing, he pulled out a number of items from the portmanteau. The red slippers could stay – at least they fitted. But what would a lady wear with them? More red, he supposed, and the only scarlet outfit he could find turned out to be perfect. Whoever it belonged to was obviously tall herself, and the man was little more than a skeleton after the meagre rations of the last few weeks, so he slipped into the dropped-waist dress with ease. A wide band of ermine ran around the hem between his knee and his ankle, matched by the deep cuffs and edging around the neck, so only a small length of bandaged leg showed above the tops of the red slippers. He might get away with people thinking they were stockings.

His head, however, was a different matter. It was the one area where he hadn't been able to bear removing the original bandages, so they were now stained and frayed. He would just have to make sure that as little of his face showed as possible. Finding a hat in black silk, he wedged it down low. Next he turned up the ermine collar on the dress so that it covered the whole of his neck and some of his bandaged chin. He felt his face carefully. With the dust-covered glasses on to protect his sensitive eyes, only the very tip of his nose, a cracked upper lip that still bled occasionally and the middle of his cheeks would be visible. Powder. He needed powder. With a hooked finger, he tipped the grey dust from the little pot in the travelling wardrobe into his other hand and then patted his face with it. At least the bandages would not glow with pristine whiteness now.

Although the Lord only knew, he must make a terribly ugly woman.

There was no time for wardrobe improvements however. The hook was descending again. He stepped quickly from his own crate, climbed up on to a neighbouring carton, and grabbed hold of the swinging hook. Whoever was hauling it from above saw the line jerk and started to pull, and the man held his breath, lowering his face. Up, up he sailed, towards the light, trying not to look, or be seen. He couldn't ask anyone for help. Not yet. Perhaps not ever. He was on his own.

After a couple of agonizing minutes the hook finally swung clear of the trapdoor, and for a moment the man was suspended between the deck and the hold. Before the stevedores could see what was going on, he leaped from the hook as nimbly as his ragged feet would allow and hurried to the side of the boat, where he leaned as gracefully as he could, trying to act naturally. Nobody seemed to have seen what he'd done, so he scampered to the gangplank and followed the last of the passengers on to the shore.

England.

This was his own soil. He could sense it with his very being. But it wasn't home yet. He only had one name to go on, one possibility of a starting point.

So he waited patiently in the shadows, until he caught sight of his crate being offloaded. Slipping through the straggles of people greeting their loved ones, peeping through a handkerchief held to his face, he kept close and watched three huge men man-handle the portmanteau into the back of a black and shiny van, and then quickly pulled himself in beside it.

She felt like home, somehow, this lady of the bright costumes and feathery headdresses. Through her clothes, he felt that he had come to know her. And soon he would find her. He smoothed down the label on the side of portmanteau, finally able to see it now it had been released from the crate:

Lady Diselda Bootle-Cadogan (née Carruthers)
Lowmount Hall
Lowmount
Hampshire

14

Jack didn't want to open his eyes after a very fitful sleep – at least he assumed he'd been asleep. Granny Dazzle had been of teaching him poker, floating about his room on a coffin carried by Ozzy and Ice. As both of those things seemed entirely possible after what he had witnessed the previous night he was no longer entirely sure what was real and what was not.

There was a noise above his head. Breathing. Jack's eyes flew open; to his astonishment, there stood Bone, mere inches above his face and holding a blade across his throat in a very worrying fashion. 'Bone, no!' he shrieked.

The valet blinked his violet eyes, offended, and Jack wished he could swallow back his words. Every morning, for as long as he could remember, Bone had come into the room to lay out his clothes for the day: the dressing gown on the valet stand so he could run down to breakfast; school uniform pre-scrumpled on a chair;

sports or swimming clothes packed into a suitable bag. How could he ever have imagined that Bone might ever intend to hurt him? Besides, Jack recognized the blade. It was the cut-throat razor that Bone had used the previous evening. And when Bone passed him the small bronze hand mirror, Jack's heart sank.

It was back.

The hair on his face was thicker than ever. And it wasn't just a beard. His eyebrows had fantailed up and out, and the curls on his head had darkened and descended, meeting to form a band of blue-black bristles across every millimetre of his forehead – a monobrow gone wild. Hair spurted out in tufts from either side of his eyes, and his cheeks, chin and neck were covered in a thick matting of the same blue-black colour. Jack peeked under the bedclothes. 'Thank goodness!' he yelled. Below the collar-line his skin was the same pimply white flesh as normal. Then he peered more closely into the mirror. Was it just the hair in his eyes, or were his lips and the tip of his nose turning dark blue?

'What's happening to me, Bone?' he whispered.

Bone shook his head sadly, then rapped his knuckles against his pale skull as if trying to knock a memory or two out of his ear. When nothing happened, he shook his head again, then held up the razor for Jack. 'Sir?'

'Oh! Yes. Yes, please. Get rid of it.'

Fifteen minutes later, Jack's skin was smooth and dewy once more, although the strange colouring on his lips and the end of his nose still remained. Bone studied them anxiously for a moment, then held up a finger. Motioning to Jack to stay put, the man scuttled out of the room.

'Don't you worry, Bonio,' said Jack wearily. 'I'm not going anywhere looking like some black-make-up-wearing gothy Emo kid.' His parents would have a fit. They'd have his name down for Eton, and probably therapy, before the morning was out. He smiled wryly at the thought.

Fortunately for Jack, Bone had ready access to Granny Dazzle's collection of pots and powders, so when he returned it was with a thick panstick that turned Jack's nose and mouth back to flesh colour, and then a tiny hint of orangey lipstick to try to make his lips look normal again. Jack stared unhappily in the mirror. Was this any better? 'I look like Michael Jackson.' Guisely . . . Jack groaned. Guisely would see in detention that he had make-up on, and then he'd take vast amounts of pleasure in making Jack's life absolute hell.

'Should I tell Mother what's happening? Get her to take me to the doctor's maybe?' She could take Ozzy at the same time, have them inspect his holey skull . . .

Bone considered this for a moment, then shook his head, tapping his temple with one of his skeletal fingers.

Jack sighed. 'You're right. She will think I've gone mad. Have me locked up. And then I'll never find . . . oh!'

Ozzy and Ice. Where were they? Jack checked his watch. Just time to get down to the museum and possibly the crypt before breakfast. He certainly didn't want the strange duo turning up at school again. 'See you in the dining room, Bone,' he said quickly, swinging his legs out of the bed and seeing with great relief that they looked as sparsely haired (and long and gangly) as ever.

He scooted along to the museum, checking his reflection at intervals. The make-up was only noticeable when his face was completely still and shoved up close to the surface of the vase or whatever it was he was looking in. So there was the solution. As long as he kept his face moving – talking, perhaps – nobody would be able to see that he was wearing lipstick and old-lady slap. He'd try it on Ozzy and Ice.

But the twins still hadn't returned. Jack scoured every inch of the museum, even looking down the throat of the stuffed bison. Well, they were a peculiar pair. Who knew where they might have got to? He sprinted along to the family crypt, half hoping that the smoky Granny Dazzle might be back, in case she could shed some light on what was happening. But she too was absent. Jack kicked the stone sarcophagus crossly.

'Why aren't you here? I need you, Granny Dazzle. Look!' And he thrust his face up to the plaque with her name on it. Jack was appalled to see at first glance that the blue-black facial hair was already growing back only minutes after his shave. 'I am hairy and blue, Ozzy and Ice turn up and then just as mysteriously disappear, and you appear all ghostly and prance around on top of your coffin talking about museums. It's weird – all of it.'

But if Granny Dazzle had anything more to say to him, she was apparently not going to do it now. Jack apologized for kicking her and trudged back to the little museum. He looked long and hard at all the strange artefacts behind the glass, interesting to him alone – her clothes, her mementos of her long-dead husband, family hand-me-downs like the pair of stupid old scales in honour of his Libran star sign. What had she wanted him to find here?

And as soon as that thought appeared Jack realized his mistake. 'It's the wrong museum,' he said softly.

Their so-called museum was more of a big souvenir cupboard. Other people – normal people, Jack thought longingly – probably had similar shelves at home with stuff from Disneyland on it and straw donkeys from Spain. It wasn't a proper *museum*, and it wasn't the right museum.

Jack raced off to breakfast, grateful for the very first time that it was set out formally on a table the size of a tennis court. His parents would never see his make-up from their end. Just to be sure, he waved toast around in front of his face and munched wildly, acting on his theory that the black lips shining through the orange lipstick would be less visible if they were moving. He was just about to make his escape when Bone came to the door with a message on a silver salver. He looked whiter than ever.

113

Lady Bootle-Cadogan read it quietly, then crooked an eyebrow at Jack. 'You've made a friend,' she said, not sounding terribly pleased about it. 'Two friends.'

'No, I haven't,' said Jack.

'Well, there are two of them at the door and they want to cycle to school with you.'

Jack's heart leaped into his throat. Ozzy'n'Ice! It was a huge relief that they'd shown up at last, but coming to the door and introducing themselves to Bone . . . no wonder he looked a little unsettled.

'I'll go and talk to them,' he said before his mother could ask Bone to bring them into the room, and he scampered off along the corridors, feet slithering on the polished wood, his toenails leaving long scratches along the grain . . .

He skidded to a halt at the door. 'Oh! It's you.'

Gouldian Finch shoved his hands further into his pockets and nudged the broad hulk of a boy straddling the bike next to him. 'You OK, B-C? Your lips look a little strange. That's not . . . lipstick, is it?'

'It's jam,' said Jack quickly. 'What are you doing here?'

'Helping you fit in, like you said yesterday,' drawled Finch. 'This is my friend Wormwood. Wormwood

114

Moonshiner. He's starting at Clearwell today. I thought if we all cycled in together we'd be a little gang, bit of a band of brothers, and then you wouldn't stand out quite so much. In your lipstick.'

'I told you, it's jam,' said Jack, irritated and not at all sure he liked the look of Gouldian's new friend, who was staring at him with a strangely flat-eyed expression. Joggling his backpack from one huge shoulder blade to the other, he looked like Gouldian's minder. 'Thanks anyway, but it's . . . um . . . an open day at Eton, and Mother wants me to go, so I won't be at school until later anyway.'

Gouldian's beady eyes screwed up at the mention of Eton. 'Oh,' he said sniffily. 'So Clearwell's not good enough for you any more?'

'I love it,' said Jack. 'I'm just keeping my mother happy. You know what my parents are like.'

He was saved from having to explain further by Bone's appearance in the corridor behind him, Jack's uniform dangling from a hanger and the battered backpack hanging behind, as if Jack had shrivelled up inside his school clothes. 'Time to go,' said Jack with a burst of relief. 'See you at school later.'

'You bet,' said Gouldian with a tight smile.

Wormwood Moonshiner nodded in a dour fashion, and the two of them pushed off down the long gravel drive to the east gates.

'Thanks, Bone,' said Jack, whisking into a nearby cloakroom to get dressed. He called out through the door. 'I need you to take me somewhere this morning. Not school. Well, maybe later. But first I have to find a museum – a special museum that Granny Dazzle would have liked. Do you have any idea where that might be?'

Silence. Jack yanked open the door to see Bone staring at him, his expression an odd mix of understanding and bewilderment, with just a touch of sadness thrown in. 'You do know, don't you? Can you take me?'

And five minutes later the Daimler pulled away down the drive, with two words keyed into the satnav.

'BRITISH MUSEUM.'

15

BC1. There were times, Jack decided, when owning a Daimler with a very short registration plate had its advantages, and driving through London was definitely one of those times. Tourists obviously thought they were some kind of royalty, or possibly stars making a film about royalty. Some tried to peer in at the windows, nudging each other and giggling but generally falling out of the way – perhaps because Bone looked fairly terrifying, hunched behind the wheel like a vampire seeking his next victim, or maybe because Jack was so clearly not either of the fair princes, William or Harry. The police, meanwhile, seemed to believe they were visiting dignitaries; at one stage, somewhere around Kensington, they even pulled out all the stops and surrounded them in a cavalcade which would have made the Queen herself bleary-eyed with pride.

So much for being ordinary.

But it was very useful that they were able to drive

straight to the front entrance of the British Museum on Great Russell Street. Bone slung the Daimler on to the yellow hatch markings, and nobody so much as pipped a horn in their direction.

'Right, wait here for as long as you can, and if you have to move just drive around until I find you,' said Jack, shielding his eyes from the flash of cameras from some nearby tourists. Bone simply nodded, pulling down his tinted glasses, and Jack raced out of the car.

As he ran through the doors into the main foyer it occurred to Jack that he had no idea what he was doing here. 'This had better be good, Granny,' he muttered under his breath. 'I need a big clue . . . very soon.'

But he needn't have worried. As soon as he looked around Jack knew perfectly well why he'd been sent here. The place was in uproar. The souvenir shop had been completely ransacked; two ladies wearing neat blue tabards were scurrying left and right, trying to piece together the broken shelves and stop the gaggles of schoolkids from looting mementos. The security guards, meanwhile, were barking at each other through walkie-talkies as they cordoned off the whole of the left-hand side of the foyer area with yellow tape.

'Weird little kids, I tell ya,' yelled one of them, cuffing a teenager who was staggering out with a massive stone bust of some pharaoh or other under his arm. 'Yeah, one was sort of green. Big eyes, both of them, made up like that Eye of Horus in the Egyptian room. They went through the whole of room four, blowing up the display cabinets somehow, and then they disappeared upstairs.'

Jack's heart sank. Sort of green . . . big eyes, He craned his neck to hear.

'Yeah, police on the way, and we've closed down the whole section. What? . . . Yeah, Egyptian Death and Afterlife.'

Jack swivelled on the spot as police sirens wailed outside. He could still see the Daimler; Bone seemed to be driving it backwards and forwards in some random formation, meaning that the police cars couldn't get near to the building. Time! He was giving Jack time.

He skidded across to a nearby floor plan. 'Egyptian Death . . . Egyptian Death . . . upper floor, room sixty-two.' The lift was just beyond the decimated souvenir shop, but even as Jack turned towards it, a security guard dragged a security barrier in front of the double doors. 'Everybody leave the premises, please. All visitors to leave the museum now.'

'No can do, Mr Guard,' muttered Jack. There was no way he was leaving Ozzy and Ice in whatever mess they were in upstairs in Egyptian Death. Time for his years of training in the special Posh With Dosh sport of Hall-Running to come into practice.

He took a step back, tutting as if he was disappointed at having to leave. Then, as the security guard looked around at the police storming in through the doors, hurling abuse at the idiot in the Daimler out the front, he backtracked through the trashed souvenirs, then pelted around the bookshop to the far corner, barely faltering on the shiny foyer floor. East Stairs. That was what he wanted. Just as he was spotted by a nearby guard Jack bolted through the doors and ran like he had never run in his life. Up the steps, two at a time, sometimes three at a time, bashing into the walls as he took the corners, tongue lolling as he started to pant, head down and nostrils widening as he tried to work out where he was. Then suddenly he saw the sign saying UPPER FLOOR and flung himself past it.

Room 62 was just along on the right. Even if the little map hadn't shown him, he would have guessed where his friends were by the odd green light emanating from the doorway. He gathered his breath and ran on in great, lolloping strides, his feet seeming to go faster than he could handle, so much so that it was easier to steady himself by touching his knuckles to the floor every so often. At the entrance he skidded to a halt, stuck out a hand and swung himself around the door jamb into the room.

It was a disaster area. Swirling green gases obscured the mess to a degree, but Jack felt his feet crunching on broken glass, and he knew that somehow the display cabinets had exploded in the same way as the ones downstairs.

Ozzy and Ice half turned as Jack shot into the room, nearly skidding into them. Both smiled vaguely at him. 'We thought it was here,' said Ozzy sadly, nodding towards the little painted figure he held in his palm, which was now most definitely the colour of a leaf in spring.

It wasn't just the green vapours that were turning Ozzy the colour of a vegetable. His skin was deepening in colour right before Jack's eyes. If he got hairier too, like Jack kept on doing, he'd turn into the Grinch. 'You thought *what* was here, my little . . . uh . . . green friend?' said Jack, glancing nervously over his shoulder

121

as the unmistakable *ping* of the lift opening echoed down the corridor behind him.

Ozzy sighed. 'My missing piece. So we could help you more.'

'Help you we could,' echoed Ice, shaking her head. She took the figurine from Ozzy and handed it to Jack, along with the information card that had sat alongside it.

Jack blew grey-green dust off the statue. It was a mummy, wearing a crown that fanned out from the head like the sun, and it held a shepherd's crook in one hand and in the other a big . . . whip, he supposed it would be called.

'Why would your crown be here?'

Whatever country these two came from, they had some seriously funny beliefs. He read the wording on the explanatory card aloud: '*The God of the Under-world, Osiris, along with the embalmer god, Anubis, are entreated by the scribe Hunifer to grant him unre-stricted access to the realm of the dead.*' He looked at the children. 'Is that supposed to mean something to me? Because it doesn't.'

Ozzy gazed at Ice for a moment, looking sudden-ly much older than his ten years or whatever he was;

looking, in fact, as ancient as ancient could be. An arctic chill ran down Jack's spine, so intense that he felt the hairs on the back of his neck lift. When Ice nodded slowly, Ozzy said, 'The evil Seth had a chest made for me, and in it I died.'

'Died he—'

'He did – yeah, I get it,' said Jack, his neck still prickling uncomfortably.

'Isis –' Ozzy pointed to Ice – 'found my body so that my soul could be saved, but Seth discovered it and had me chopped into pieces and flung across the world. We thought this wooden statue was the last piece.'

'It is not the last piece,' said Ice with a wobbling lip.

Ozzy nodded gravely. 'The last piece it is not.'

'This is . . . this is nuts! It has to stop.' Jack shuddered involuntarily from the tip of his nose – now clearly black again, he could see in the glass of the one remaining cabinet – to his tail. Bottom. Backside. Jack glanced around. Why had he thought he had a tail? If he did, it wasn't poking out of his school trousers, and thank goodness for that. He gave himself a quick shake and turned back to the duo as the ruckus along the corridor increased in volume.

Ozzy was staring at him with great anguish, and Jack felt his pain more than his mother's in any conversation with her about his not going to Eton. Disappointed, the expression said. You've let us down, Jack. We came here for your help and you're turning us away. Ice's eyes had frosted over so completely they were chips of pure sapphire, and Jack shuddered again. If what they had said was true, even partially true, then these two were very powerful beings. And he'd just ticked them off in a major way. He backed off a little.

But how could it be true? It was rubbish, surely. Ozzy and Ice were claiming to be Egyptian gods, murdered and drowned and chopped up and flung about in bits . . . that just couldn't be right. His thoughts were interrupted by the security guards tramping down the corridor, shouting, 'In here!' and, 'Back up! There's three of them!' It was only a matter of moments before they were all arrested.

And Jack decided he had to trust them. They'd come to him for help. Now he needed theirs. 'OK, Ozzy'n'Ice and Ice'n'Ozzy, if you're who you say you are, it's time to prove it. Because in . . .' Jack lifted his head and sniffed the air. The scent of the nearest guard was wafting around the corner, mingled with the faint aroma of extinguished cigarettes and sweet wrappers. It was the one who'd moved the barrier in front of the lift. 'In ten and a half seconds those guys with the big sticks and walkie-talkie thingies will be in here. Cause a diversion. Blow something else up,' he suggested helpfully, snuffling over his shoulder as the source of the scent drifted ever closer. Then he checked himself – was he *smelling* someone's arrival?

Ozzy smiled. 'There is no need.'

'No need is there,' sparked up Ice.

The boy, who now looked rather more like a wizened little old man, crossed his arms over his chest, uncannily like the wooden figurine that Jack still clutched in his hand. He put it down hastily, and looked upward to see the source of the breeze that was tickling his curls. 'A ma . . . A ma . . .' he spluttered.

To Jack's astonishment, a magic carpet was descending from the airspace near the high ceiling. Only it wasn't actually a carpet – it was the camp bed covered by the red altar cloth.

Ice beckoned to Jack as the contraption rattled to a halt at their side. Jack leaped on to the middle of the bed, clutching the frame in terror as the guards screamed around the corner. Ozzy and Ice stepped regally on to either end as it lifted gently into the air, the boy with his arms still crossed, and Ice with her arms aloft and poised as if she was carrying an invisible water bowl on her head. As the guards skidded straight underneath and crashed painfully into the shattered remains of the Egyptian Death and Afterlife displays, the magic camp bed floated out of the room, up through an open skylight and out into the cloudy sky.

Jack winced as he peeked over the edge of the bed. He'd done skydiving once, but he'd had a parachute attached to his back for that rather than relying on a length of hundred-year-old canvas and a patched altar cloth to keep him aloft. But the flight was smooth. Pleasant even. Ozzy and Ice certainly seemed to be enjoying it; both were standing with their eyes closed tight and their faces into the wind.

Fumbling in his pocket with one hand, and hanging on tightly with the other, Jack pulled out his mobile phone. The signal up here should be amazing, he thought. He punched the first number on his speed dial. 'Um, Bone, I think I found what I was looking for. I've got a ride home, so . . . meet me after school, will you? Oh, I'll be a bit late because I've got detention again.'

There was a long pause while Bone loosened his jaw, and then Jack heard the affirmation: 'Sir.' It was followed by a peculiar creaking sound.

Jack frowned as he hit the end-call button. If he hadn't known better, he would have sworn that Bone was . . . laughing.

16

'What the blazes are you doing?' shrieked Lady Diselda.

The young man hesitated in the doorway, his hand over his chin so she wouldn't be alarmed by his bandaged face. Actually, he was far more frightened of her than she of him.

Lady Diselda backed away towards the fireplace and picked up a candelabra. Not that again, thought the man. He'd thought she at least would be different.

'There is so much occurring that is strange. My husband's mutilation and death. The undertakers moving outside the village and changing their name. Young Albie. And now you. You're wearing my dress. And my hat. And those glasses – they're . . .' She shoved the candelabra in his direction. 'Take them off. NOW!'

The man winced. But he knew it was now or never. He reached up to his face and pulled off the dust-encrusted glasses, exposing his weepy eyes to the dusk.

'Goodness, you're crying.' Lady Diselda lowered the candelabra as she peered at him closely. 'And those eyes – they're extraordinary. I still don't think you should have been wearing my darling Jay's glasses, but . . .'

Rummaging in the folds of her dress, she pulled out a handkerchief and passed it to him, exchanging it for the glasses. 'Please don't cry. I'm not that horrid, really, even if everyone around here thinks I am.'

The man blew his nose and then wept some more from the pain of it.

'Oh, look at you.' Lady Diselda's voice softened. 'You poor dear. You're all covered in bandages. Did you . . . ? Do you need my help?'

The man nodded and shuffled forward. With a slight frown, Lady Diselda drew him into the room by the hand, staring up at him with a hint of shock in her eyes. 'Why – you're . . . you're a man!'

He shrugged, then nodded, which caused the hat to slip down over one bandaged ear.

Lady Diselda took a deep breath and then removed it.

'Let's get these dreadful bandages off, shall we?'

With a gentleness that he would never have

expected, the young woman unwound the top bandage. He heard her intake of breath as she glimpsed the horror beneath it, but she carried on until his whole face was exposed. It didn't hurt, but when she turned him gently towards the mirror, he struggled to hold back his tears once more.

He was completely white. His hair had virtually disappeared, and the few strands that remained glinted silver in the moonlight. His skin gleamed with a ghostly pallor, and a pair of strange violet corneas gazed back at him above the ermine collar.

'You're albino, yes? Someone threw you out because you're albino. That's tragic. How mean. And you borrowed my clothes and my husband's glasses and even – yes, even the heart locket I gave him – from my portmanteau to dress yourself.'

It wasn't that far from the truth, so the man nodded. He couldn't remember the rest of it properly anyway, even if he wanted to correct her.

'Can you speak?'

The man shrugged, his eyes watering again.

'Your name. Can you say your name?' said Lady Diselda gently.

Unhinging his stiff jaw, the man tried to say the

only word he knew he could manage. 'Home,' he droned, but his lips didn't make the right shapes. It didn't sound right, even to him. 'HOME!' he tried again, more insistently, but Lady Diselda put a finger to her lips and then took his hands gently into her own.

'I hear you. Bone. Your name is Bone. All right then, Bone, you will stay here with me, and nobody will bother you again for being different. I'm different too. We'll look after each other.'

With a decisive sniff, she gathered up his discarded bandages and seized a couple of the most lurid dresses from her portmanteau. 'From now on, Bone, these are museum pieces. It's time for a change. The clothes of a respectably widowed lady for me, and the black garb of a personal butler for you. Are you with me, Bone?'

Forever, he wanted to say. Her strength, her enthusiasm, her sheer exuberance was highly infectious, and as he nodded the man tried to laugh. It hurt like the devil, and erupted in a horrible keening sound that made the lovely Lady Diselda blink, but it was a start.

17

Jack finally settled on a cross-legged position with a hand on either side-rail to allow himself a comfortable journey on the magic camp bed. He couldn't see much as he'd had the foresight to point out that they might attract even more police attention if they swooped around above the M4, and Ozzy had obligingly enveloped them in a cloud of pale green smoke until they burst through the clouds. It was probably just as well though, Jack thought. The ground, when he'd chanced a glance over the edge, was a very, very long way away.

The green gas meant that Ozzy and Ice were also impossible to see – or hear, as they rushed through the wind. Questions about the figurine and their strange story would have to be suspended until later. As the word 'suspended' floated across Jack's mind he let out a yelp. 'School! I'm supposed to be at school. I've got detention later, and if I don't turn up I'll get . . . I don't know, another one!'

There was no response. Jack shuffled his bottom awkwardly along the bed and tapped Ozzy on the shoulder. The amber eyes loomed at him through the wispy gloom, and Jack pointed towards the ground and shrugged. 'Where are we?'

'We are home,' intoned Ozzy proudly. Ice's squeak was just about audible from the back of the stretcher, but as Jack knew she'd only be bleating, 'Home we are,' he didn't bother straining to hear her. Stirring with a long-nailed finger, Ozzy created a whirlpool in the yellowy-green gas; at the bottom of it, magnified somehow, Jack could see the spires and crenellations and the glint of the puddle in the rooftop pool of Lowmount Hall.

Jack blew into the smoky spiral, widening the view. 'It's not bad, is it?' he said with a modest grin.

Now that he could see his home, his estate, his future, from the air, he couldn't believe he'd never asked his father to bring him up in the helicopter. As well as the Hall itself – a mini-castle really – he was also treated to a grandstand view of the grounds immediately surrounding it: the north view leading down to the limestone folly that one of his ancestors had built in the 1700s, complete with fake Roman

133

columns and grapevines made of stone; the south-facing lawns on which an enormous rock concert had been hosted a couple of years before (which Jack had not been allowed to attend); and the rolling fields to the west, dotted with little outbuildings, including Bone's cottage, the service road passing over a little bridge with a cattle grid to the graveyard, and the chapel. Jack took a closer look. Somewhere beneath those fields was the secret tunnel. *His* secret tunnel. For some reason, that gave him more of a sense of pride than the whole of the rest of the magnificent estate.

But then he saw what was beyond the trees. School. And . . . 'Nooooo,' groaned Jack. 'The Clearwell Comp Comp trials. I'm missing them!'

As the ground grew closer he could see the tables laid out at the start of the cross-country route. Kids surged around them, signing their names, checking their trainers, pinning a numbers to their chest. Even from the sky, Jack could spot the hooked nose of Gouldian Finch and the massive hunched shoulders of his horrible new sidekick, Wormwood Moonshiner. Gouldian was whipping his head around, looking for something. Some way to cheat, probably, thought Jack.

'I have to get there now!' Jack stabbed a finger at the

scene below them. 'It's my one chance to be normal. Only . . . no! Wait!'

Normal. Right. Just how normal would he be, descending from the heavens on a flying camp bed flanked by a green boy and an ice-eyed girl? Ozzy seemed set on giving him a regal landing. They were aiming for a spot right next to where Guisely was chewing the end of his pencil, his moustache worrying away at it like a small, lead-eating rat. Clearly the green boy hadn't heard his desperate change of heart, so as soon as they were near enough, Jack hung off the side of the stretcher bed and dropped into the tops of the poplar trees.

It was a painful descent, bouncing heedlessly off branch after branch, sharp twigs inserting themselves up his nose and into his ears, the ground leaping up towards him in several scary snapshots until finally it was immediately below him. He landed with a thump on one side, and lay there for a moment, too stunned to move. 'Owwwww,' he whimpered gently, but a pistol crack soon brought him to his senses. They were off! And he was still a good two hundred metres from the starting point.

Leaping to his feet, Jack raced through the trees

135

as fast as was humanly possible. No. Faster. As trees zoomed by in a blur he became aware that the trestle tables for signing up were right ahead of him. Already! His Hall-Running training had paid off. As he screeched to a halt Jack grabbed the pencil from where it drooped on the lower lip of Mr Guisely's open mouth, and scribbled his name on the form. 'Who . . . what the . . . why . . . ?' babbled Guisely, staring from Jack to the pencil and back again.

'Sorry, sir, bit late,' panted Jack, suddenly conscious that his tongue felt too big for his mouth. 'See you in detention later!' he added cheerfully. Then, grabbing the square of cloth with his number on it, he headed out after the others.

He was a good four or five minutes behind. Furthermore, he was having a bit of trouble making out the coloured flags that indicated the way. There were a couple of blue ones that were easily visible, but he missed the next one completely, mistaking it for a great big leaf. Realizing his error, Jack headed back and held the flag up to the light. The instructions on the sign-up sheet had said the flags were blue. This one was definitely green.

For a moment he stared around him, disorientated

and not a little miserable. He was ages behind now. He had no chance of getting a place in the heat, which meant he wouldn't qualify to be in the Comp itself and would never earn himself enough cool points to be considered normal. And then he'd never convince his mother he fitted in and he'd have to go to Eton, just like that. In his frustration he felt like ripping the green flag to pieces, as if it was the cause of all his problems.

Just as he raised it towards his mouth to shred it with his teeth, a scent curled up to his nostrils. Jack sniffed. 'Finch,' he growled. Gouldian Finch and his henchman had been this way first. That must be what they'd been doing – changing the flags from blue to green so that anyone running behind them couldn't see the way!

But Jack wasn't beaten yet. Because, unwittingly, the boys had left a far clearer trail that would lead straight to them. With a victorious shout, Jack sprang off towards the next green flag, following Gouldian's oily stench and Moonshiner's musty, metallic tang. He was back on track instantly, loping between the trunks of the trees, hurdling roots like one of his family's champion racehorses, covering ground so fast that once again he dropped his hands to the earthy floor to keep his balance, and on he ran, sniffing, scenting, panting, almost bursting with joy. He could still win this!

At one point the path crossed a brook, and the scent disappeared. But it didn't matter. Jack could hear them now, Gouldian rapping out orders and Wormwood lumbering along like a T. rex, which was just what he looked like when Jack rounded a copse of trees and found him stumbling helplessly around, his short, stubby arms stuck out straight in front of him like a sleepwalker, zombified like a mummy . . .

Jack could bear it no longer. 'Moonshiner, I know what you're up to!' he yelled.

Wormwood's squat head jerked in Jack's direction. He looked a little bewildered, and Jack realized that effectively he was only Gouldian's hired help. Finch was organizing the cheating all on his own. There was a shuffling in the undergrowth ahead of them; Jack turned and ran towards it, vaulting above the ground in an impressive spring that had him thinking he should consider high jump as well as cross-country. Then, arms and hands and fingers extended to full stretch, he prepared to tackle the odious Finch head-on. 'Cheat!' he bellowed, a martial-arts expert flying through the skies . . .

Only just as he was about to make contact, the figure shrouded in the undergrowth shifted backwards. Missing his footing, Jack sprawled to the ground, and at the same moment the sun went out. Jack's head whipped around, and his heart sank as he thought about what might cast such an impressive shadow. A magic flying camp bed, perhaps?

He hardly dared look, but as soon as he did he instinctively raised his hands to his face, yelping as they made contact with the end of his nose far sooner than they should have done. It wasn't the camp bed – the shadow had been caused by an enormous bird of prey, which was now trying to peck off his doggy nose! Jack almost let it. Perhaps it would be doing him a favour.

But then a voice thundered from the bushes close to where he lay tangled in branches. 'Get up, Jack.' It was an order, not a suggestion, issued in a smooth, majestic voice. 'Get up now! Run. Run as only you can!'

The next instant he was on his feet, his eyes on a level with the terrifying talons of the huge hawk that was about to carry him off as nest-fodder. Jack acted instinctively, jumping up and poking the bird in both eyes with forked fingers. 'Leave me alone!' he barked. With a startled caw, the hawk wheeled away, and Jack took the opportunity to spring out of the bushes and hare after the scent of Wormwood Moonshiner. Who had that voice belonged to? He sort of knew it, he was sure, but it sounded so powerful, all rumble and echo. And where was Gouldian Finch? It had to have been him in the bushes, but now he was nowhere to be seen.

The scent was strong again. Jack lunged forward, running, carried by the joy of the feeling of power coursing through his limbs, switching course as the smell of Finch and Moonshiner grew woolly and another sharp, dark tang took over, which could only be one person, the person who counted most at this moment . . .

Guisely! There he was, by the finish line, still chewing his pencil. No, realized Jack. Smoking! He was having a sneaky cigarette before the first runners came in. That was the scent he had recognized, the vile stench of Guisely's horrible habit. Anyway – he'd done it! He was first back to the finish!

But just as he loped through the last of the trees, a body hurtled out of nowhere, flat out, and in a slamming of limbs Jack found himself on his back on the ground beneath a nasty, snarling face.

'If you've cost me this race, I'm going to kill you.'

Jack leaped to his feet and held out his hand. 'Minty! I'm really, really sorry. Didn't see you there . . .'

Minty was juddering from head to foot with barely controlled fury, but as she scrambled to her feet her expression turned to revulsion. 'Posh, is that you? Man, you're even weirder than I thought. What's happened to your face?'

'My face?' said Jack, bewildered, alarmed that any minute now more racers might come tumbling through the trees.

With a speed that made him jump, Minty snatched the square of cotton that was pinned on his chest and thrust it into his trembling hand. 'Cover yourself up, freak,' she said with a sneer.

Perplexed, Jack stared down into a puddle, and his breath came out in one shocked wheeze. He couldn't speak. His nose had grown longer, and blacker. The tips of his ears, now black, were peeking through his ridiculously thick hair. And, worst of all, the hair didn't stop at his forehead. Instead there was a full coating of short black bristles over every square millimetre of his face.

He started to say something to Minty, but she just

141

lifted her hands. 'I don't want to know,' she said. 'Just make sure I win this race, OK?'

'Yes! Of course. I'll . . . you know . . .'

Come last, he thought. Lose. How could he approach the table looking like this anyway? All hopes of ever fitting in were sinking straight into the ground. He could almost have cried. Jack lifted up the cotton square with his race number on it, about to do just that, when the scuffling of trainers on leaves caused his ears to twitch. Twitch? 'Oh, please don't twitch,' he begged.

But suddenly his competitive spirit took over. He hadn't won; Minty was already shaking Mr Guisely's hand as though it was a wet fish. But he could still come second. And as this was only a heat, that would be enough to win him a place in the final Comp itself.

He sprang forward just as Gouldian Finch and Moonshiner drew up behind him. The finish line was ten metres away. Eight. Before Guisely could see him clearly, Jack held his number up directly in front of his head. 'Forty-two! I'm in! Second!'

He skidded to a halt, burying his face in the square, pretending to wipe away sweat. Guisely sniffed. 'I could disqualify you for taking off your number, Posh Boy,' he said, but he didn't sound very convincing.

Jack rubbed his face some more, his voice muffled by the cotton. 'Oh, ha ha ha! You're a big kidder, sir. We all know that's not in the rules.'

He tugged his fringe down furiously and peeked at Guisely over the top of his makeshift mask. The teacher stared suspiciously, then jerked his head. 'All right. Second. But don't think that gets you out of detention. Or you, Minty West!'

But Minty had already slouched away. Before anyone could see his hairy face and his . . . well, it was more of a snout than a nose . . . Jack pulled his T-shirt over his face in a footballer's victory pose, and sauntered off after her. Normal, he told himself. Just act normal, he repeated, as he blundered blindly into an oak. 'Oops! Tree.'

Normal? Fat chance, Jack thought with a groan. He was getting less and less normal by the second.

18

The man who now called himself Bone settled quickly into life at Lowmount Hall with Lady Diselda, who seemed to have little more idea of how to conduct herself than he, always getting into trouble for her brutal honesty, her non-stop chatter and her hare-brained schemes. She was as lively as he was silent. A perfect match.

Lady Diselda spent the first few days at the Hall cutting off ties with the other staff and introducing Bone as her personal valet – an old family retainer who had been released to her by her aunt's death, she said, her eyes daring anyone to question her. Bone himself squirmed uncomfortably whenever she introduced him as 'our old family servant'. He didn't feel old – not inside, where it mattered. He felt like a young man. Certainly young enough to be devotedly in love with this woman who had been kind enough to take him in.

But the mirror showed the reverse. He looked old. How old, nobody could say. In some ways, he was as hairless and smooth-skinned as a newborn baby, but only because his skin had flailed off and grown anew in whatever terrible accident it was that had brought him to the hospital. His sad purple eyes would follow Lady Diselda around the room as he realized again and again, with fresh pain every time, that she would never look at him as anything other than a servant. A freakish one, at that. But deep down he knew she was better than that. She deemed him her friend, and her friend he pledged to be.

Generally his appearance still frightened people, so he kept out of sight and was happy to do Lady Diselda's bidding. By the second week they had fallen into a routine: breakfast first, then Lady Diselda's visit to the local children to tell stories and encourage them to learn a few more letters and eat some fruit, with Bone listening through the window; lunch followed by some activity outdoors – archery, or horse-riding, or just sitting in a field doing some sketching, or arranging untidy posies with which to decorate Lady Diselda's quarters. All the time Bone listened, and nodded, and tried to improve his voice, which remained obstinately cracked and broken. It mattered little. Lady Diselda could talk enough for both of them.

One day, she took him hunting, her last opportunity before her growing belly would prevent her from riding for a few months.

'Come on, Bone,' she called as he bounced painfully along on the horse that had belonged to Lord Jay. 'The boar will be long gone at this rate.'

Suddenly she signalled to him to stop and slid from her horse. With a glint in her eye, she cocked the rifle against her cheek and motioned further along the track. There it was, snuffling and foraging in the undergrowth – a massive, hairy wild pig.

Bone took one look at it and screeched at the top of his hideous scratchy voice. 'Home! Home! Ho-o-o-me!' His panic disturbed his horse, which reared and bucked as if he'd stuck it with a bayonet. Bone clung on, arms around its neck, terrified that it might toss him into the path of the vile creature ahead of them, even more afraid that the thing might hurt his beloved Lady Diselda.

And suddenly he saw what he had to do. With one hand he gripped the neck of the horse, so that instantly it calmed and fell under his command; with the other he leaned around and scooped up the unsuspecting Lady Diselda, who in her alarm fired off a shot into the forest that sent the pig scarpering.

'Home, home,' bleated Bone, clutching the lady in a very unseemly fashion across his saddle, conscious that he must avoid any hurt to her swollen stomach, that he should get away from that . . . that thing in the forest . . .

He steered the enormous horse through the trees, fingers entwined in its mane while his other hand held Lady Diselda effortlessly in place, and emerged from the forest with a shout of triumphant laughter that sounded like a donkey braying. Slowing the horse, he carefully let Lady Diselda slide to the ground and then jumped down beside her.

She brushed herself down quietly. And then she thumped him. 'What on earth do you think you're doing? You could have killed us all.' She put a trembling hand on her stomach. 'I could have shot you, or myself, and my horse is still in there, for crying out loud. It was just a boar, you idiot. A little piggy!'

The man stared at her. A little piggy. That's all it was. What had got into him? His eyes pricked with looming tears, when suddenly he heard a funny sound. He looked up to see Lady Diselda's dancing dark eyes, her pearly teeth gleaming as she leaned on his horse and laughed until she was hiccuping back her tears.

'Bone! Oh, Bone, you are hilarious.'

He chanced a small smile, despite knowing that it risked making his face look like a sick ventriloquist's dummy, and she prodded him in the side and laughed some more. 'Rescuing me! That's what you were doing, isn't it? Saving me from the nasty piglet. Oh, dear, sweet Bone.'

She mopped her tears of laughter with a delicate handkerchief, then handed it to him. After blowing his nose loudly, he handed it back to her, and then she screamed with laughter. 'Bone, my dear friend. Promise me you will never leave me.'

Never, he wanted to say, my heart is yours forever. Instead he nodded, and patted her shoulder so clumsily that her knees buckled.

'Those hands, Bone – you have the strength of a thousand men in them. Be careful.' Lady Diselda looked around. 'Well, I suppose I'd better go and rescue Pickle,' she said. 'You stay here until I get back. Don't want you scaring off the pig again. Or was it the other way round? Anyway, when I return, there's something special we need to do.'

Special, thought Bone. He liked the sound of special. Entwining a finger into the horse's reins, he leaned against the fence to wait for his beloved mistress, shifting carefully under the canopy of trees to keep the sun off his skin. When Lady Diselda took a few minutes to return, he glanced around at his surroundings.

He was standing next to a small, neat garden, which bordered a whitewashed cottage. It was nice. Comforting. But then a woman came to the front door brandishing a broom, and Bone's pleasant mood disappeared.

'Away with you,' hissed the old lady, shaking the business end of the broom at him. 'I know what you are – don't think I don't! My William will be home soon and then we'll see you off properly.'

Albino, he tried to say, shaping his mouth into the syllables, just albino, but of course the word wouldn't come out, and when he tried to lift his hand to calm the woman down she shrieked at the top of her voice: 'William! William, come quick. The monster's finally come!'

Bone shook his head as a young man in a dark suit came charging around the corner. Not monster, he wanted to say. Just Bone.

But the boy and his mother were now approaching, the lad shouting something at him that appeared to be a prayer. They really did think he was a monster! And they were going to kill him, with no more consideration for him than they would have given the boar in the woods. He was simply pestilent vermin that the village should be rid of. With a muffled moan, he cowered behind the stallion just as a large scythe loomed up over the horse's saddle . . .

'Mrs Waite, no!' cried Lady Diselda, bursting from the trees.

'But look at it!' screamed Mrs Waite. 'The monster has finally come.'

'Yes, and we know what to do – when the monster arises to spread its pestilence and make us all as undead as he,' shouted her son, laying a calming hand on his mother's arm. 'We've been preparing.'

'Yes, let us deal with it!'

Lady Diselda dismounted quickly. 'This is not an "it", Mrs Waite,' she said gently. 'And he is certainly no monster. This is a person – my good friend, Bone.'

The woman faltered and fell back, and then William stepped up to the fence. Shaking, he put out a hand. 'Ever so sorry, Mr Bone. We're a bit . . . a bit at sixes and sevens. William . . . Waite, at your service.'

Bone stared at the proffered hand for a moment, then shook it as gently as he could. Nevertheless William winced and nursed his hand a little as he tucked it behind his back. 'Please forgive my mother,' he said urgently as the woman behind him dissolved into tears. 'We lost my brother recently. She's not been the same since.'

Bone tried to smile in sympathy, then realized that might terrify the woman still further, so instead he nodded politely and stepped back behind the horse. He could understand that – not being the same. He wasn't the same either. 'I'll explain about the Waites on the way home,' Lady Diselda whispered. 'I was just about to anyway.'

She took both sets of reins in her hands, nodded wordlessly at William and his sobbing mother, and with Bone dodging the shafts of sunlight by lurching spikily hither and thither, they made their way back to the Hall.

19

It was midway through the afternoon, hardly worth going into school properly. Jack decided to go home and get some help with his appearance, then go back for detention. He'd been excused from the day's lessons by an email from Bone, informing Clearwell Comp that Jack was having root-canal work on his canines.

Jack ran his tongue along his lower teeth as he loped back to Lowmount. Then the upper. Then he moaned. His canines were indeed enormous. Dog-like. He wished he actually *was* at the dentist, having them pulled out. And where were his strange little glowing pals and their magic camp bed when he needed them? Bone wasn't answering his phone, though Jack would have been very glad of a lift home. He was tired after all that running. Dog tired. Argh!

After a while he broke into a trot, trying to avoid being distracted by the enticing scents drifting up from the surrounding trees and plants – cat, and hedgehog (which made him turn a little giddy and run around in circles, squirming in the dirt for a moment, but he couldn't see the prickly creature and so eventually remembered what he was meant to be doing). Most of all, what he could smell was other dogs. No! Not *other* dogs. Just dogs. 'I'm a boy,' he told himself. 'Not a dog. A normal boy. Well, maybe not normal but . . . yes! A normal-ish boy.'

At length he emerged from the hedgerows behind the tall limestone columns of the folly and took a quick glance in the ornamental pond before it. He was still hairy. Still long-muzzled and dark. Still very much a freak, he was sad to observe. As he rubbed at a patch of the coarse black hair on his cheek Jack stopped and looked at his hand. 'Well, at least that's not hairy.' It was a bit of a funny colour, slightly bluey-black, as if he'd been rolling in dirt. But then he remembered that he *had* been rolling in dirt, at the near-delight of finding a hedgehog, and couldn't decide whether or not remembering that made him feel better.

One thing was certain, however. He could not go into detention – or anywhere, for that matter – looking like this. With another deep sigh, Jack tacked up the sloping ground towards the Hall. Inside he scooted down the corridor, trying to turn back as soon as he heard the ominous click of his mother's heels on the parquet flooring. It was too late. She'd heard him.

'Jack? Is that you? What are you doing home?' *Click click. Click click. Click click click click click.*

She was nearly upon him. Jack felt at his face in anguish, then grabbed the helmet from a nearby suit of armour. He shoved it quickly over his ears and rammed it down, the visor not quite closing over the extra length of his nose. Leaning against the wall, he raised a hand nonchalantly as his mother loomed into view.

'Jack Algernon Bootle-Cadogan, what on earth are you doing?'

Think, Jack, think, he told himself. 'Just popped back for this,' he said thickly, pointing at the helmet. 'We're doing the Civil War in history; thought I'd show everyone an original Royalist helmet.'

'Oh, Jack!' His mother hurried over and cuddled him to her cashmere cardigan, nearly causing Jack to gag at the overpowering aroma of Hermès perfume. And at being clutched to the bosom of his usually cool and distant mother. 'You've never shown any interest in our heritage before. Furthermore, I wouldn't have thought the hoi polloi at Clearwell would be at all into it. How lovely!' She rapped his visor. 'It might be better to hand it around though, not wear it. Take it off.' And she started tugging at the helmet to prise it from his head.

'No!' shouted Jack, holding on for dear life. 'Get off! There's . . . another reason! I've . . . I've got . . . spots! Huge ones!'

'Oh, poor Jack. We all go through it, darling.' Lady Bootle-Cadogan let go abruptly, then peered through the slot in the helmet. 'I do understand, you know. Is there a special young lady we're trying to impress?'

Jack sighed. This was one of those awful questions that didn't have a right answer. If he said no, she'd make him take the helmet off and then all hell would break out. If he said yes, she'd want to have some talk or other with him – about the importance of marrying someone in 'their' class, or, worse, about boys and girls and birds and bees. With a trip down to the stables to talk about where the foals came from . . .

But even that, as hideous and unthinkable as it was, did not compare with the enormity of her discovering the truth about what was under the visor. Taking a deep breath, Jack uttered the only female name he could bring to mind. 'Yes. Minty West.'

His mother nodded knowingly. 'Ah, Minty West. She sounds sweet.'

Sweet? She was about as sweet as Wormwood Moonshiner.

But Lady Bootle-Cadogan was smiling indulgently at him. 'Well, you look very cute in your helmet. She'll adore you.'

Shoot me now, thought Jack, rolling his eyes behind the visor. Jack waited until she'd clattered off along the corridor in search of a National Heritage lady to terrify, then he punched Bone's number into his mobile and fed the phone through his visor. 'Meet me at the graveyard gates in ten minutes,' he said, the metallic ring of his voice echoing inside the helmet. 'And bring the razor! We have a hair situation. Repeat, a hair situation.'

Time to check in on Ozzy and Ice, assuming that they'd come home after dropping him at the Comp. They seemed to be the Wardens of Weirdness, after all – perhaps they could explain a few things to him, to follow up on their revelations at the British Museum.

Jack raced into the room, trying not to salivate out

of the visor. 'It's like the core of the earth in here,' he panted. 'I'm boiling! And I can't seem to sweat properly – it's all dripping off the end of my tongue. Water!'

Ice and Ozzy were still standing on either end of the camp bed, even more statue-like than before. Their features seemed to be smoothing out, changing, so they appeared more serene somehow. As he entered the room they stepped down calmly, and Ice laid a hand on his head. Jack cooled down instantly. Ozzy, meanwhile, pointed one of his long curly fingernails into a bucket; it quickly filled with water. Jack gasped, not knowing whether to stare at the bucket or at the finger. It was completely green now, no hint-of-a-tint about it. Then again, he himself was now bending over the bucket and lapping from it, sticking his great floppy tongue out through the slot in the helmet. So who was he to stare?

When he had drunk his fill, half emptying the bucket and slopping the remainder on to the floor with his clumsy licking, Ozzy nodded to Ice. They stepped to either side of the door with the weird eye, holding their arms aloft like the assistants on a gameshow.

'It is time,' said Ozzy.

157

'Time it is,' agreed Ice, her eyes sparkling with delight.

'Is it? Time for what? Time for you to tell me what's going on, perhaps.' Jack folded his arms sniffily, feeling suddenly rather cross about all the mystery surrounding him, and the fact that his dog-like head was now stuck fast inside a Cavalier's helmet.

But Ozzy was shaking his green dome of a head, pointing down the tunnel to the crypt, and as Jack watched, to his utter astonishment, a figure appeared in the doorway, glistening, smiling, and then half evaporating before gathering to a more substantial image before him. 'G-Granny D. . . . '

His grandmother's ghost floated sadly across the museum floor, wispy, diaphanous, shimmering and fading before his eyes. Jack wanted to give her a hug, make her laugh, but the hand he put out passed straight through her middle, and he withdrew it quickly.

Not that it seemed to have bothered Granny Dazzle. Maintaining her sad smile, she began to turn until she was spinning, rising, her feet enveloped in flame, just as when she'd appeared to him in the crypt. Then suddenly she slowed down, stared straight at him and threw back her head.

158

Jack was reminded of Bone unlocking his jaw whenever he tried to speak. The apparition of Granny Dazzle rotated gently before him, her head tilted backwards, her mouth wide open, and her finger pointing towards the back of her throat. 'You want . . . you want to say something?'

Jack almost laughed at his grandmother's familiar look of impatience. No. That wasn't it. Then she was off again, spinning and flipping her head back and forth and pointing at her mouth. 'Thirsty? You need water. I've got a bucket here – I could tip it . . . No! OK.'

This time the sad eyes positively snapped with frustration. She whirled before him, exposing her ghostly epiglottis as if she was chomping on an invisible apple, but Jack was completely stumped. He stared and stared and then shrugged. 'I'm really sorry, Granny Dazzle. I don't know what you mean. Unless . . . is it something to do with me turning into a dog?'

At that Granny Dazzle abruptly stopped turning and nodded.

'OK, OK, and is it something to do with dogs being able to see ghosts and things, like you always believed your sheepdog Bonza could do?'

Granny Dazzle half nodded, then waggled her hand left and right. Sort of.

'Right, so . . .' Jack thought hard. 'I can see you because . . .' It was a horrible, terrible thought, but Jack had to know – '. . . because I'm turning into Bonza?'

The ghost's moan was almost a squawk. He was clearly way off the mark. Granny Dazzle threw both translucent hands up in the air and then began gesturing towards her mouth. She beckoned to the bewildered Jack and drifted back into the tunnel. Jack followed, hearing the clunk of Ozzy closing the door behind him, glad for his extra doggy-vision in the darkness.

But when he opened the crypt door that Granny Dazzle had just floated through, Jack nearly fell over. The place was packed. Standing room only, and many of those people – or ex-people – *were* standing. On Granny Dazzle's sarcophagus, on each other's shoulders, in some cases *in* each other's shoulders as their smoky, silvery forms blended into each other. There had to be thirty or forty ghosts in total, Jack reckoned.

The moment they saw Jack, the throng of apparitions shimmered and started to spin.

'N-now, hang on,' he stuttered. 'It was all right when

it was just my own great-grandmother, but who are you lot? You're a bit scary, all clustered together like that.'

Granny Dazzle was obviously in charge. With a quick wave of her ghost-hand, she summoned their attention, which was when Jack noticed a particular ghost with a familiar-looking set of super-long ear lobes . . . 'Johnnie with the Ear Lobes! You're all my relatives! My dead rellies!'

To a ghost, they all nodded. And then, before this information had a chance to sink in, they started to spin again, whirling and weaving in and out of his vision behind the visor, dropping their jaws and pointing . . . pointing at their mouths. 'Not this again! But I don't know . . . I don't understand . . .'

He didn't like it, the way they were all writhing around like that. Now they were melding into one waxy candle of ghost, spinning and spinning, flames licking at their feet, and their horrible, sometimes toothless, old mouths turning into one giant open red cave with a great big finger pointing at it, filling the room, pressing against him, enveloping him inside the vapours . . . just so he'd *really* get whatever charade they were trying to act out, he supposed. But he didn't. He still didn't get it.

Jack was suddenly desperate not to be sucked into the smoking column, eaten up by that greedy scarlet mouth. He fought his way through, scrabbling madly, until finally – finally – he reached the far side of the crypt, threw open the door to the graveyard and scrambled up the steps; sunlight flooded the crypt and the ghosts immediately evaporated. Leaping over the graves of Bill the Gardener and Vera the Organist, Jack hurtled to safety, to the strange, silent man at the edge of the graveyard, standing without expression, a cut-throat razor ready in his hand.

20

Lady Diselda led Bone through the corridors of Low-mount Hall, careful not to disturb any of the rest of the ageing family members who were littered about the staterooms like cats dozing in the weak afternoon sunshine.

'I wanted it in my own quarters,' whispered Lady Diselda as they arrived at their destination. 'The old lady insisted it belonged here, with the rest of the family heirlooms. I told her this was just my wedding portrait and I didn't give two hoots about the rest of the family being able to see it, but they overruled me. As always. Thank goodness you're here to support me,' she finished with a slight smile, pressing his arm.

Bone stared at the portrait, still aware of the feeling of warmth on his sleeve where her hand had lain. This family made him cross, very cross, with their instant dismissal of anything Lady Diselda had to say. She was right – this was private. The emotion in the portrait was so raw that Bone felt he really shouldn't look, but she was gazing up at it now, her dark eyes shimmering with tears, which she shook back determinedly. Just to be polite, he straightened his new tinted glasses and studied the portrait closely.

She had looked beautiful on her wedding day. She looked beautiful every day, of course, especially as the birth of her child grew ever closer and her skin glowed with whatever it was that nature bestowed on it at such times. But in the portrait, clinging to the man she had made her husband, Lady Diselda looked like an angel. Forthright, feisty, perhaps even a little frightening, but an angel nonetheless, in her cream silk column dress with the daringly high hemline, the diamond-encrusted circlet of silk around her head, the outrageous huge white heron feathers that would have overpowered anyone less striking.

'So that was my Jay,' she was saying now, and Bone turned his attention to the proud, upright young gentleman with the handlebar moustache. He wanted desperately to feel jealous of him, but somehow he could not. Instead he felt only kinship, an unmistakable closeness.

'Wasn't he dashing?' Diselda whispered, and Bone nodded.

'Lord Jay was the only man I will ever love. He had my heart on a string, you know – the necklace you took from my portmanteau. Actually it was just a locket with a tiny seed pod inside it, but I treasured it, and he loved it.'

Bone's hand crept to his throat. He remembered the necklace. Remembered his shame that she had found him wearing it. Though she was wrong, wasn't she? He'd had it in the hospital; he hadn't pilfered it from the portmanteau. It had always belonged to him, he was sure of it . . . Now she held it out to him.

'A beggar woman gave me the locket – I call it my heart. It was at the site Jay uncovered. She said it would protect the family from a curse until the day I die! Rubbish, of course. I put seeds in it from the tamarisk tree, my favourite tree in the whole world. I wanted to plant it with Jay, but he's gone now. We could do it now, if you could help me . . .'

Nodding, Bone felt his spirits rise. She wanted to do this with him! That was their special task. When Lady Diselda saw his agreement, she laughed. 'I wish everyone here was as understanding as you, Bone.

Come on!' And she skipped off to her quarters to find a trowel, Bone following at a respectful distance.

By the time he caught up with her, she was on her knees before the portmanteau, dragging items out into her lap and spreading them around her. 'See this,' she whispered with a wrinkle of her nose. She held up a letter. 'Jay gave me this on our wedding day. He . . . he had the feeling he might be in danger. He and Albie had just found what they believed to be the final resting place of Osiris, God of the Underworld. The Egyptian authorities were really quite cross about it, as he discovered when some threatening fellows turned up at his poker game.' As she tipped the envelope up five cards tumbled out on to the floor. 'He had to cheat, so he could finish the game quickly and get out of there alive. This was his winning hand.'

Bone picked up the cards. Four jacks, two black and two red, and the Queen of Hearts.

'Very special cards,' said Diselda. 'And not just because I was his Queen of Hearts. Take another look.'

Obediently Bone fanned the cards across his palm. It was a reasonable hand, but not a brilliant one. A royal flush would have beaten it. He certainly couldn't see anything special about it. And then it hit him. The two red princes! Both belonged to the hearts suit. It was an incredibly risky cheat. Jay must have been desperate, very sure that his life was in danger. And suddenly he remembered . . .

'Bone, what is it? You look most peculiar.'

He couldn't tell her, of course, because he still couldn't speak and, besides that, he wasn't really sure how he could express his feelings. But . . . somehow he knew, just knew, that he had seen this poker hand before.

Lady Diselda tugged the cards out of his hand. 'Strange, isn't it? He really took a chance. But then that was my Jay. And that's why they tried to kill him,' she added softly, a lone tear following the curve of her cheek. 'They all said it was a scorpion bite, but he'd already warned me he was in trouble. He got himself to hospital, you know. Someone had tried to . . . to cut out his heart. He took himself off into the desert to die. So I didn't even have a body to mourn, anything to . . .'

Dropping creakily to his knees, Bone patted Lady Diselda on the back, almost shoving her inside the portmanteau as he did so.

'Sorry, Bone. I mustn't get emotional. I knew what

he was like when I married him. It was worse for those poor people you met today: the village undertakers. Albie was Mrs Waite's son, barely seventeen at the time, for goodness sake. So bright and curious, and he begged Jay to take him along on the dig. So he did, and he got himself killed. Or worse. Mrs Waite has been in the most dreadful mess ever since, talking of monsters and all sorts – you heard it for yourself. They've even insisted on changing their name so nobody can find them. It's dreadful. Especially as . . .'

Diselda busied herself with the locket to avoid Bone's eye. 'They never found Albie,' she said quietly. 'The authorities in Egypt may have him still, because they say . . . they say he was the one who murdered Jay . . .'

But Bone had almost stopped listening, her earlier words floating around his head as isolated memories began to hum and make connections in the very centre of his brain. Unwittingly his hand drifted to his chest, to the ring of blood that was still impregnated into his skin, the stain that had never come off, no matter how often he tried to bathe it away, wincing at the terrible, stomach-churning tenderness of his flayed skin.

Now he knew why. And in the same moment he understood why he loved the young woman before him so devotedly; why he'd felt so at home in the village of Lowmount and the estate that watched over it; why he recalled the poker game and the hand that had saved him from death, from damnation . . .

His heart. Someone – this Albie, perhaps – had attempted to uproot his heart from his body. But it had beaten too strongly, and it had drawn him back here.

'Home . . .' he moaned softly.

More than his home. His estate.

For he was Lord Jay.

Possibly missing a vital organ or two. But Lord Jay all the same.

21

Jack ricocheted off gravestones as he stumbled across to Bone, whose lilac eyes flashed with alarm as he brandished the razor defensively.

'Bone, be careful. You'll have someone's eye out!' screamed Jack as he slithered unsteadily to a halt. 'It's me. I've turned all weirdy beardy again, and now this helmet's stuck over my muzzle. Nose, I mean.'

Bone threw the razor into the car and hurried over to him. Exhausted, Jack collapsed on the grave of one PINKY BARTHOLOMEW, QUARRYMAN AND DEAR FAMILY MAN, his black-tipped nose projecting from the visor like a submarine missile.

'As if I'm not freaky enough!' squeaked Jack in despair. 'A hairy face and seventeenth-century armour rammed on my head. I'll have to live off soup for evermore! And I hate soup – it's not even real food.'

Bone crouched down slowly before him, his ancient knees snapping like firecrackers as he took a gentle hold of the helmet. Through the visor Jack could see the purple eyes studying the iron-work carefully; then, with one swift move, Bone yanked and the helmet came off.

For a moment Jack wondered if his head was still inside it. He couldn't hear or see anything, and it took a while for his senses to readjust to being out in the open. When he managed to focus, he stared at the helmet pieces in Bone's hands. Far from wrestling it off his head, it seemed the manservant had quite simply ripped it in half. 'Oh my life!' he said. 'You must have hands of steel. What's Mother going to say? I'll have to weld it back together . . .'

Bone was silent, but then Bone was always silent, so Jack wittered on about the consequences of going home with a broken family antique, until finally he realized that Bone was even more silent than usual. He couldn't even hear the man's usual raspy breathing. The old valet was staring at him, head cocked, his strange slash of a mouth opening and closing, not as if he was trying to form words but as if he was miles away . . . years away, even . . . certainly not there with Jack, in the graveyard in Lowmount.

'Er, Bone, are you OK?' Jack took the torn helmet

pieces from the manservant, and prodded him softly in the chest. It was as if he'd electrocuted the man. With a speed that belied his great age, Bone leaped to his feet, groping at his chest and grunting madly to himself.

'Bone, I promise you, it's all right!' Jack got to his feet too and followed Bone in his skittish dance through the graveyard. 'It is just me, honestly. I know I look like . . . well, I'm not quite sure what I look like . . . but it's just me, really it is . . . Bone, wait!'

The poor man was in the midst of some dreadful memory and was thrashing around in the bushes like a maniac, groaning his own name over and over again. Something else was bothering him – the sight of Jack's hairy head must have triggered a memory from his past. Jack had never seen him so discomposed. In fact, he'd never seen him discomposed at all. Ever. Now that the tables were reversed and it was up to him to look after Bone, he had no idea what to do.

Then he remembered Granny Dazzle's lullabies. For years Jack had imagined they were for his benefit, but one evening, looking up from his bed, he had realized he wasn't the only one who was soothed by them. Bone had been stretched out like a plank across the wooden chair in the doorway, snoring like a road drill.

Scampering over to Bone, he cleared his throat. 'Please forgive me for not doing this as well as Lady Diselda,' he said, and then he began to croon in his most calming voice:

> 'Hush little baby, don't say a word,
> Granny's going to kill you a mocking bird,
> And if that mocking bird won't sing,
> Granny's going to give you a heart on a string.
> And if that little heart breaks free,
> Granny's going to grow you a tamarisk tree,
> And if that great old tree falls down . . .
> You'll still be the cutest little lord in town.'

Jack held his breath. He couldn't remember any more. In fact, he was quite amazed he'd recalled the verse right up to the end, as he was often snoring away just as much as Bone by the time the great old tree was falling down. But luckily his lullaby had already had the desired effect; Bone was swaying gently in the bushes, definitely lulled.

'Out we come,' said Jack softly, tugging on Bone's

173

coat-tails and coaxing him back towards the car. 'There we are. Nothing wrong now. Apart from my . . .' He checked his reflection in the side mirror, and nearly cried. 'Apart from my dog-head,' he finished.

Bone gave himself a shake as Jack stared in the mirror. 'I *am* a werewolf!' he moaned. 'Wait – I can see my reflection, so I can't be!'

Bone gazed at him thoughtfully, then shook his head, sticking a finger beneath his top lip on either side of his mouth and making biting movements. 'Oh,' said Jack, 'you're right. It's vampires who have no reflection. So I am a werewolf.'

Bone was shaking his head again, this time pointing up towards the pale sunshine leaking through the clouds. 'Right – werewolves only come out at night. Something to do with the moon, isn't it? But . . .' In for a penny, thought Jack. 'I thought ghosts only came out at night too, and I've just seen a whole bunch of them in the crypt. I know it sounds mad, but Granny Dazzle was there, and lots of my old ancestors. Even Lord Johnnie with the Ear Lobes.'

At this, Bone's mouth flopped open and he started to hyperventilate once more, so Jack burst hastily into song again until he'd calmed down. Then he opened the car door, retrieved the razor and handed it to Bone, reclining the front passenger seat fully to turn the Daimler into a makeshift barber's shop. 'I've got detention,' he said, 'and I can't let Guisely see me like this. But there's lots of stuff I need to tell you, Bone, even apart from me being a ghost-seeing dog-thing. I'll fill you in when I come home again.'

Bone scraped away at his face for a good quarter of an hour, twitching Jack's head this way and that with the end of a skeletal finger. When he'd finished, Jack knew from the valet's expression that he wasn't going to like the result. He sat up and tipped the rear-view mirror in his direction. 'I'm blue,' he said despondently. 'Less hair, or what I suppose I'm going to have to start calling *fur*, for crying out loud, but my nose is still all stretched out, and my skin is –' he stared at the reflection of each cheek in turn – 'blue. Blue as the seven seas.'

And he let out a long sigh. Guisely was going to absolutely slaughter him. The best he could manage by way of a disguise was to wear his baseball cap pulled down as far as it would go, and then drape the cotton square with his running number from each ear like a sort of veil. It looked appalling, but less strange than his shaved-naked-dog appearance.

It was a good job he had some form of disguise though, as school was madly busy. 'There must be a function on,' said Jack to Bone, staring at the foyer which positively thronged with people. 'Open day, perhaps.' The mere thought of it reminded him of Eton, and his mother, and the Clearwell Comp Comp . . . Jack checked his watch. 'I'm late! Guisely will definitely kill me now.'

His running skills were called for once more. The entrance hall was far too packed with people for Jack to break through quickly, but to his enormous delight he found one positive aspect to the disasters of the last few days: he no longer needed his map, because he could *smell* his way to wherever he needed to go. Skirting the main building, he pelted around the gymnasium, following Guisely's scent mingled with . . . it was so disgusting he hardly dared to think of it . . . his own smell from when he'd been to detention the previous day.

''Scuse me,' he said, head down, pushing past the strangely dressed men and women, boys, girls, babies in prams . . . multitudes crowding the corridor. Maybe it wasn't an open day but a meeting of local amateur dramatics groups, judging by the variety of costumes. It wasn't until he turned around in the classroom to close the door behind him that two things struck him. Firstly, the man wearing tights and a long flaring top on the other side of the glass was staring right at him, opening his mouth and pointing down the back of his throat. And secondly, although he'd just pushed straight past him and the people around him, Jack had never felt a thing . . .

'Nice of you to turn up,' said Guisely. 'Though I'm beginning to think you must have some kind of death wish. Nobody could seriously be so stupid as to turn up to detention dressed like a cowboy. Is this some kind of joke?'

'No, no,' said Jack. 'Just thought costumes were the thing, you know, like all those people outside.'

Guisely pushed past him and stared through the glass. 'Which people?'

Jack lifted a hand and was about to point. Not that he should need to. The building was bursting at the seams with people, in all manner of dress, all waving at him, all doing fish impressions at him through the glass, all looking directly at Jack. Then he realized. 'Nothing,' he said quickly. 'Nobody. Nothing.'

He was the only one who could see them. It was possible that he was the only one that they could see too. Certainly all their open-mouthed attention was focused on him as they peered through the classroom door. Guisely was still studying him with an unusual amount of interest . . . and Jack realized he needed to explain his disguise. 'Cold!' he yelled. 'I've got really nasty germs. This is like a . . . a surgical mask. Don't come near!'

Guisely paused, then cocked his head towards the desks. 'I don't know whether to pity you or hate you, Posh Boy,' he sneered. 'All that inbreeding must have messed with your brain. Just sit down, anywhere, and keep yourself occupied for five minutes. I have to go and find the rest of them. And don't –' he pushed his nose up against Jack's in a cloud of nauseatingly stale smoke – 'move. An. Inch.'

Guisely stared him down one last time, before wheeling around and striding off down the corridor on his stumpy legs. 'Bet you never do any Hall-Running,' muttered Jack.

Suddenly his eyes lighted on the computers against

the back wall. Five minutes, Guisely had said, collecting 'the rest', whoever they were. He quickly logged on to the Internet.

At home the computers were solely for the use of the Hall, to advertise open days and National Heritage times and persuade people to get married or hold concerts in the grounds. Homework, his parents insisted, should be done the old-fashioned way – with straining eyes, in the head-crushing quietness of the library. Jack was always a little startled and then utterly grateful at the speed at which a computer could provide him with information. Although it wasn't nearly so much fun as swinging along the library walls on the great lengths of library-ladders-on-rails . . .

'Ozzy and Ice,' tapped Jack into a search engine. He was still wondering about the strange story they had told him at the British Museum. 'Nope. That's not right.' There was a site for an Australian ice hockey team, a video of a large schnauzer eating ice cream and several million entries for Ozzy Osbourne. Jack stared hard at the dog. It was blue-black, just as he was beneath his running-number veil . . . was he a schnauzer too?

But he was getting distracted. Jack racked his

brains, trying to remember what the children had said their real names were. Osiris! That was one. Holding his breath, Jack clicked on the search button, and the screen reeled before him. 'Forty-nine thousand entries! I haven't got time to read forty-nine thousand entries!'

But after he'd read three, he realized they all told the same story, and it was a familiar one. Osiris, the Egyptian God of Agriculture and Fertility and various other things including the Underworld, was murdered by his brother Seth by being suffocated in a crate. His body was rescued by his sister-wife Isis, then cut up and thrown across the planet by Seth so that Isis had to run about trying to collect the bits. 'OK,' murmured Jack. 'Osiris and Isis. So that's who you say you are, weirdy twins. Weirdy *married* twins, if this is right. And I suppose the missing bits would explain the hole in Ozzy's skull. But why do you think I can help?'

Jack flicked back to the schnauzer video clip. It looked somewhat like him, but a lot more cuddly. His hand crept under the cotton square and touched his chin, then quickly withdrew. The hair – FUR – was back. Maybe he was an . . . Egyptian werewolf? From his personal knowledge of werewolves, which was pretty much entirely based on Professor Lupin in *Harry*

Potter, they became monsters because they were bitten by another werewolf. And then they bit other people. Well, he certainly didn't feel like biting anyone, and he hadn't been bitten himself . . .

'I *was* bitten! Blackie!' Quickly Jack dragged up his sleeve. The pinkish mark was still visible. Excited, he whisked back to the computer and typed in 'Dog . . . Egypt . . . graveyard . . .' before smacking enter. 'Dogs of Ancient Egypt,' he read. 'Jackals were known to prowl around graveyards . . . yes!'

Footsteps were approaching. With his acute hearing, Jack figured they were still two corridors away. 'Jackal,' he typed in, tapping his feet anxiously. There, on the screen before him, was a picture of Blackie, or rather a pack of Blackies, snarling and salivating and looking distinctly hungry. 'All right, my little Egyptian friends, let's see how we fit together,' he said under his breath, entering the words 'Osiris Isis jackal' into the search box.

He was still staring at the screen when the door opened behind him. Jack peered into the reflection in the computer screen, but even the sight of Guisely approaching across the classroom, flanked by Minty West, Wormwood Moonshiner and Gouldian Finch, wasn't as panic-inducing as the entry he had just read.

And as Guisely reached for his shoulder Jack sprang out of his seat and launched himself out through the window beyond. When he vaulted some fifty metres through the air before coming to the ground, Jack knew that he'd definitely discovered his new identity.

Anubis, Guardian of the Dead.

The jackal-headed god.

Son of Seth the evil.

Doghead.

22

From the moment he had realized his true former identity, Bone made a promise to himself.

He would never tell.

The shock to Diselda, his beloved, his darling wife, would be too much to bear. Not to mention the scandal, the upheaval, the unearthing of all the old mysteries surrounding his death. They'd even held memorial services for him, for goodness sake.

He would maintain his strange appearance: keeping to the shadows, avoiding sunlight, sporting his tinted spectacles so people didn't stare at his violet eyes. He could manage it as long as he was in a position where it was permissible – no, advisable – to blend into the background; almost, really, to be invisible. He would be a servant, not lord and master of the estate.

So the exterior he could work with. But what of his damaged interior landscape – the rolling dunes of sand that were all he could picture unless something triggered a rare spark of memory, the arid stretches of nothingness that should have been filled with laughter and excitement and discovery, but which rang only with silence and discontent. No. He loved Diselda too much to burden her with his broken soul and ripped-out memories. As a servant he could remain close to her, serve her always, and her family, until the day his body was no longer willing to put one painful club-like foot in front of the other along the corridors of Lowmount Hall . . .

And so the months drew on, the space where his heart was supposed to be filled instead with eternal devotion. Occasionally Lady Diselda shared her favourite stories about the dear husband she had known for far too short a time, and he made them his own. Their first meeting, when he had attended her dancing performance and fallen irrevocably in love with her; the poker game where she had waited outside with a carriage to spirit him away to safety; her wedding day, when he had presented her with the wonderful feathered headband, which she now displayed in her own little museum and which she wore so proudly in their wedding portrait. Each of the memories merged with wisps of the same notion in Bone's head, and he knew without doubt that he was right to claim them.

And then had come his son, the young lord, John Albert Bootle-Cadogan – called Johnnie or Jack for his father, and Albert in honour of Albie Cornthwaite, to whom Jay had been such a loving and brotherly mentor. Bone couldn't bear to get close to him – his own son. How could he ever explain his past, how he had come to be Bone, the manservant, instead of Lord Jay? Filled with love for his wife and aching with the guilt of having left her, he stayed in role the whole of Johnnie's life. And, despite his mother's best efforts, Johnnie grew to be a bit of a rogue anyway, not entirely someone that Bone could approve of, with his rather cruel, dismissive nature and his unnaturally long ear lobes which he used shamelessly to get whatever he wanted – sympathy, laughter, women . . .

In time, Johnnie went on to have his own family: the money-grabbing Jackson Aloysius and his little sister, Dolly Veronica. Jackson was stolid and unenterprising, trying to bolster his way in life by making a profitable marriage to the daughter of a banking magnate; Bone had come to have more admiration for Jackson's wife than for his own grandson. It pained him to admit it, but the Bootle-Cadogans had not all inherited the greatest of family traits. Bone witnessed all their evils and foibles at first hand, inveigled as he was into driving them around and supplying them with whatever their hearts desired. No, not too fine at all . . .

. . . until Jackson became a father, to Jack Algernon, who was without a doubt Bone's favourite of all the sons, because he grew more like Diselda and himself every day. Kind. Brave. Open – sometimes too honest for his own good.

As Bone drove away after dropping his dear Jack at school for detention he could hardly believe how much time had passed since his return to Lowmount – how many generations, how many births and weddings and anniversaries and, inevitably, deaths. At each the local undertakers, the Waite family (once so cruel to Bone but now indifferent) officiated with their usual efficiency and their odd little rituals. Always the same – payment in cash and in a strange selection of livestock, with a receipt using foreign terminology that Bone recognized a little – something from his past as Lord Jay, author, adventurer, tomb raider.

Death was part of life. He of all people knew that.

But when Lady Diselda passed away peacefully in her sleep Bone felt his innards crumble, his very spirit seeping away into the coffin along with her body. She'd wanted, had always planned, to be buried in her wedding outfit, but the current lady of the house had refused, insisting that Diselda 'at least greet her eternity with a bit of dignity'. Dignity? Bone had wanted to roar. She had more dignity in her tiny little toe than Jackson and his wife had in their entire beings. But of course he had simply inclined his head, unhooked his jaw, and croaked, 'Ma'am,' in agreement.

Otherwise, the funeral arrangements had gone to plan. The formal appearance suited the Bootle-Cadogans' rank in society. The undertakers, still headed up by the terribly ancient Wee Willie Winkie Waite, had coated the underside of the coffin in copper as directed, and embalmed the body as always, and had led away the sheep and goats that Bone had provided for them beside the graveyard. And then Jack – young Jack, who was so like his great-grandmother, so extraordinarily kind and forthright – had made exactly the speech that his Granny Dazzle would have wanted. It was all as it should be. Even though she'd moved on and left him behind, and his poor serrated chest ached at the mere thought of it, it was a fitting ending for her.

But now her beloved boy Jack was tortured. Turning blue-black. Getting hairy. Becoming a freak – a fate Bone understood only too well. And now claiming to have seen the ghosts of Diselda, and Johnnie, her son – or rather *their* son. Not settled. Not united in harmony. But instead they were half-dead, as Wee Willie had warned them all those years ago. Seth, unleashed, would hold them back from the release of death, keep them undead, as his servants. It had sent Bone into a state of such disquiet that he'd lost track of where he was in the graveyard.

It was too, too awful. He couldn't bear to think of Diselda distraught, roaming the afterlife, begging for help. He would gladly have followed her there, and had even thrown himself off the crenellated turrets of Lowmount Hall in an attempt to do just that, although he had more or less bounced and just picked himself up out of a bush. But how could he leave when Jack needed him so much, needed his protection?

Bone glared at his wretched reflection in the bronze mirror on his hall wall as he snapped open his jaw and screamed in frustration and helplessness, a terrible wail spewing out of him.

And then, unable to withstand the sight of himself for even one second longer, he smashed his fist through the mirror, knocking straight through into the scullery next door. He would not let Jack down. He would not. Whatever it took, he would do it. He hadn't been able to be there for his son and grandson. Their pains had been too deeply hidden. But he could be there for his great-grandson.

He owed it to Jack.

He owed it to Diselda.

Above all, he owed it to himself.

23

Jack made it home in record time, faster than even the Daimler could have travelled. Possibly faster than the magic camp bed. Cool. He could apparently run at speeds that the *Top Gear* guys could only dream of. Although, now he considered it, he was not entirely sure that he'd been running all the way, as he sailed out of the window and up over the fence and hared through the woods that ringed Lowmount Village. Sometimes it felt like he'd just stretched out a leg and pictured the next milestone – the bend in the road, the thicket near Waite's the Undertaker, the place where Blackie had attacked his throat – and *ZJZJOOOMP!* he was there.

Arriving at the graveyard, he checked his watch, the one he'd insisted on buying from the petrol station in Lowmount so the expensive Tag Heuer he'd got for his tenth birthday wouldn't make him stand out, or possibly get him mugged.

'No flipping way,' he growled in bewilderment.

The clock on the computer had registered 16.44 at the instant he'd decided to pitch himself out of the classroom window, but now his watch told him it was 16.45. One minute. One minute to get from school to the graveyard. It wasn't humanly possible. But it was becoming more and more evident that Jack Algernon Bootle-Cadogan was not entirely human. What he had to do next was work out how much of him was person, how much dog, and how much . . . although it still didn't seem feasible . . . how much was Anubis, Egyptian God of the Dead, and son of the 'rather nasty' Seth.

He got a clue when he looked up from his watch. 'Hey, back off,' he told Blackie and the other strays – jackals, he now knew – who were slavering around his knees. There was a pack of them, two dozen at least, and he half expected to be leaped on and divided out between them, but to his astonishment they let out one gigantic whimper and sat down in an obedient semicircle around him, wagging their tails and gazing adoringly up at the muzzle which protruded from his running-square neckerchief. The cotton square was snagging on his teeth. Jack tore it off his face, then ripped off his baseball cap to stop it squashing his ears. And suddenly he felt free, a surge of adrenalin bursting through his veins and, without stopping to think what he was doing, Jack threw back his head and howled to the rising moon. The jackals yapped excitedly then copied him, a Mexican wave of dog-heads spreading from left to right, a cacophony of howls rising up to the skies.

Jack stopped. 'What. The. Heck. Am I doing?' It was all getting much too weird. 'I need to go home.'

But things were about to get even more strange. All Jack had done was allow himself the merest wisp of a thought of what route he'd take to get back to the Hall – into the crypt, down the tunnel, up through the museum and then on to his bedroom – and the next moment he was standing at the crypt door.

'Huh?' muttered Jack. What had just happened? He turned back to the dog pack; they were still seated in their front-row-in-the-amphitheatre position, sniffing suspiciously at the space where Jack – clearly their leader now – had been standing just a millisecond before.

'I'm here!' he called across the cemetery. 'No! Not you lot . . .'

The graveyard was suddenly bristling with ghosts, rising from their respective tombstones like steam from so many kettles. The jackals rolled over to get their tummies tickled, gambolling joyfully among the dead. Jack finally dared to look directly at the one nearest him. An elderly gentleman, stout and with bowed legs like Mr Guisely, waved at him like an old family friend and then started flicking his ghostly dentures in and out on the end of his ghostly tongue.

Jack gagged. 'That's disgusting,' he said. But he wasn't really surprised at what came next: the shady form of the man tipped his teeth out on to his hand, gazed at them morosely for a moment as if recalling some long-forgotten memory, then turned to stare directly at Jack. He opened his gummy jaws wide and pointed down his gullet.

Rolling his eyes, Jack peered through the old man's smoky gaitered trousers at his gravestone. PERCY MULLINGER, HEAD GARDENER AND DEVOTED HUSBAND.

'Percy,' he said with a sigh, 'I'll help you find a dead dentist or whatever it is you need, just as soon as I work a few things out. Is that all right?'

Percy shook his head, his rheumy eyes glistening through the dusk as Ozzy and Ice's had once done.

The hordes of ghosts wavered in the evening breeze, all starting to rotate slowly as Percy Mullinger was doing, opening their jaws and indicating the back of their throats. Jack turned to Percy's neighbour, and quickly read the gravestone. VERA CORNTHWAITE, BELOVED WIFE, MOTHER, B-C CHAPEL ORGANIST . . .

'Um, Vera,' he said as the lady with the tightly curled grey hair (well, translucent silver, really, as was the rest of her, but he assumed it had been grey when she died, because she looked pretty old), 'thanks for coming. I can see you're all a bit upset about something –' this as the ghostly Vera clutched her ribs so violently her eyeballs slid out of their sockets and back again like a couple of jellified yoyos – 'and I am going to find out what it is you need. Yes, all of you,' he said, holding up his hands to get the attention of the spinning, jaw-dropping ghosts who jostled for space. 'I am going to get to the bottom of this, but you just have to let me find out how I'm supposed to do it. Who, in fact, I'm supposed to be. Can you give me a day or two?'

'Noooooooo!' The banshee cries of the ghosts merged into one deafening shriek. 'Noooooooo . . .'

'He is coming!' hissed Vera Cornthwaite as Percy Mullinger nodded urgently, sending his ghostly dentures flying across the plot.

'Who?'

It was difficult to make out over the combined wailing of the graveyard ghosts, but Jack thought he heard the word *monster*. Who could they mean?

'Himmm!' wailed the throng of ghosts. 'He's coming!'

They were all starting to spin together as the ghosts in the crypt had done, a murky, caliginous column of smoke from which limbs and eyeballs and teeth sprung out at intervals. Flames licked at the base of the cylinder, while the top formed one enormous cavernous mouth.

The screech of tyres at the graveyard gate snapped Jack from his reverie. 'Bone!' he cried as the valet stumbled from the Daimler, fending off the snapping jackals with great swipes of his fists that sent the dogs flying, crashing against the trees. 'Don't – they're on my side. Here, Blackie!'

Blackie scrambled back to Jack and stood,

panting, waiting for orders. 'I have to find my friends,' he shouted to Bone, who was ploughing blindly through the spirit forms. 'I think they're in the museu—'

It happened in a flash. As the word left his lips – no, as the thought merely entered his brain – Jack passed straight through the crypt doorway into the little building, along the tunnel, out through the door with the Horus eye on it, and *zzzzzip* – there he was, in the museum.

'That has got to get easier,' he gasped, leaning against the stuffed bison to catch his breath. Although what could be easier than 'think it, and you're there'? 'Bit sick-making, but pretty nifty. One of the advantages of being a dog – I mean, a god, I suppose. I wonder what other superpowers I've got?'

It was quite a moment. If only the kids at Clearwell could see him now! There was no time to ponder it, however, as he found what he'd been looking for straight away. Ozzy and Ice were hovering near the doorway on the magic camp bed, the whip and scythe in Ozzy's crossed arms brushing the ceiling, and Ice's new and rather fetching headdress crushed against the light fitting.

'There you are,' said Jack. 'I've discovered who I am, I think.' And he described what he had found out on the computer. The two nodded serenely as they drifted down towards the floor. 'And being Anubis is why I can zoom around like that?'

'It is how you travel in the underworld. You zip, we float,' said Ozzy in a matter-of-fact tone.

'OK. But I don't get why you didn't explain all this at the beginning.'

'We tried, but you listened not,' said Ozzy, his voice now thunderous. 'You would not have believed us.'

'Believe us you would not . . . have . . . do . . . done.' Ice frowned as her English escaped her for a moment.

'Maybe just one of you needs to say something – I'll get the idea,' offered Jack kindly. 'You're right though. I wouldn't have understood. And I still don't know what to believe, really, but there are these ghosts appearing to me all over the place, and they keep pointing to their teeth.'

Ozzy averted his amber gaze to Ice, who gave a little smile and said: 'They need your help.'

'Help they . . . They need your help to pass over.' Ozzy's skin glowed emerald in the dusky light of the museum.

'Pass over? Pass over what?' They seemed to have done a pretty good job of passing over their gravestones. 'Over the fence?'

'To the afterlife,' said Ice.

Ozzy smiled. 'To the underworld, of which I, Osiris, am god.'

'And I can help with that, can I?' Jack said. 'By . . . I don't know . . . checking out their wisdom teeth . . . ?'

Ice and Ozzy shook their heads, smiling at his innocence. 'No,' said Ozzy. 'Show us exactly what they were doing.'

Jack opened his canine jaw and closed it again. 'That.' He did it again for good measure. 'Just opening their mouths.'

At which Ozzy and Ice held up their hands triumphantly. 'There you have it!' said Ozzy.

'Have it you do!'

'I have to . . . open their mouths?'

'Yes. The Opening of the Mouth. It is a ceremony that you, Anubis, perform to help them pass through to the next life, to the Field of Rushes, where they can be reunited with their bodies and their loved ones.' Ice explained it all as casually as if she was telling him the way to the supermarket. 'It is simple.'

Jack whipped round to Ozzy before he could parrot, 'Simple it is.' 'No, you don't. It isn't simple. I haven't the slightest clue what you're talking about. And I think the situation is a bit urgent too.'

His strange new friends glanced uncomfortably at each other. 'What is it you are meaning?' asked Ice.

'The ghosts were pretty agitated, and they kept telling me the same thing: HE IS COMING. That is bad thing, yes?' Ice's peculiar grasp of the English language was rubbing off on him; he was talking to her like his father did to foreign ambassadors – loudly, with lots of shrugging.

But the pair were now swaying in alarm. 'Yes, bad thing.'

'So who is this "he"?'

Ozzy swallowed hard, and as Jack saw the fear etched on his green face, and the determination on Ice's white one, he was suddenly able to answer his own question.

'It's this Seth, isn't it? The guy who murdered you.' And apparently was the father of Anubis. Erk. So was Lord B-C his dad or was he the son of a murderous monster, or were they one and the same?

'Drowned me he did.'

'And chopped you up into little pieces.' Jack thought about it. My dad? Nah. No way Jackson was an evil body-chopping maniac. He didn't have the energy. So his god-dad was different to his real dad. And if Jack wasn't going to be tackling his *actual* father, he could work out a plan. 'What does he look like, this Seth monster?'

Ice and Ozzy shrugged in unison. 'We cannot say.'

'You can trust me,' said Jack. 'I'm a dog-god and everything.'

'No, we cannot say,' said Ice, 'because we do not know. We can only sense his ba.'

Jack stared from one to the other of them. 'His ba? Is that like his pa . . . his father? Or a . . . a sheep?'

He thought of the sheep outside Granny Dazzle's funeral. Was there a connection? Had he let the evil Seth trot off on four legs under his very eyes?

But no. 'His ba is his spirit,' explained Ice, smiling gently.

'A bird,' Ozzy added.

'Ah. A bird. I wonder . . .' Just hours ago Jack had been attacked by a rather large example of the bird family. 'So would Seth definitely be a "he" in this life?' he asked quietly.

Ozzy and Ice looked at each other, then shook their heads. 'Perhaps not,' said Ozzy. 'You know the ba?'

'Well, I know who might have set a big bird on me,' said Jack grimly. 'The same person who's been out to get me since day one of Clearwell Comp. Before, even. Minty We– oh no!'

Just as soon as he'd pictured the girl who'd run into him rather than let him win the cross-country race, he was zipping back through the crypt, up the steps to the graveyard and towards the car that was pulling up behind the Daimler – the car from which tumbled Mr Guisely and the dark-eyed, angry face of Minty West.

24

Bone spun round, his breath spurting out in painful bursts. Something was not right. The car that was pulling up behind contained an old foe, of that he was sure. Not just old. Ancient.

But it was only Jack's teacher – a nasty one, for sure, but just a teacher. He certainly didn't look like any kind of threat as he tumbled out of the driver's seat, screaming orders and obscenities across the graveyard, then turning to stare as the dog-headed Jack, still in his uniform, mysteriously appeared in the crypt doorway. Quick as lightning, Jack dropped down so that only the tips of his ears showed from behind a nearby gravestone, and Bone heard a distant cry of 'Err . . . Woof!'

The teacher stopped short, then hollered at the children who had clambered out of his car – a girl, thickset and dark-haired and malevolent-looking, not at all the kind of young lady that Jack ought to be associating with. Had the grace of his great-grandmother taught him nothing? Next came a boy with small beady eyes and no neck, who wore the stupefied expression of someone who'd just knocked their head on something hard. The girl, maybe. Then a younger boy. No, not younger, just smaller, with a long snooty nose held up in the air, as if there was a bad smell, and sharp shoulder blades that emphasized the narrowness of his frame.

Bone had hated them all on sight, but now he realized that it wasn't simply because he recognized the type: unpleasant, self-absorbed individuals who would pick on Jack for sport. Bone swallowed hard as once again he had the strong sensation that something was not right. A sharp ice-chip of terror was turning in his stomach, like a snowball gathering fear, getting bigger, colder, harder, becoming a cannonball. The weight of it nearly dragged him to his knees . . .

But then the teacher spoke. 'Finch, Moonshiner, seeing as you were so keen to come with me and get Posh Tosh back to detention, you go and look in that creepy building. Could have sworn I saw him. He'll be very sorry he ever scarpered out of my detention.'

'What shall I do, sir?' asked the girl, wiping her

nose on the back of her hand as the boys took off across the graveyard. 'I was keen too.'

'Sit in the car,' snapped the teacher. 'And get yourself a tissue! There are some in the glovebox.'

The girl gave him a particularly evil stare and turned back to the car, then suddenly her breath caught in the back of her throat. 'Sir,' she hissed under her breath. 'SIR!'

'What?!'

Reluctantly the teacher turned from his view of the graveyard, where the two boys were skittering down the crypt steps, and caught sight of Bone. For a second he recoiled, then he stretched up to his full height.

'Oh. You. The servant. I'm Guisely, the boy's teacher.'

Servant? Bone narrowed his eyes. Yes, he was a servant – now. But he was also a lord. An educated man. And a friend to the boy that this narrow-minded idiot was now pursuing around his own grounds.

'He jumped out of the window in detention. Didn't he, West?' Guisely looked to the girl for confirmation and she gave a surly nod. 'Can't have insubordination like that in my class.'

Insubordination? Bone frowned. The wretched man talked as if he was in charge of an army platoon, not a bunch of schoolchildren.

'So, if you'll just step aside,' continued Guisely, pulling up his too-short trousers, 'those boys will find Posh . . . I mean, Bootle-Cadogan, and we'll head on back to school to finish off detention. Then I'll think of a suitable punishment.' His ratty yellow moustache curled as he smiled with sadistic pleasure.

Humph, thought Bone. Punishment. The nasty little oik was probably sad that caning and birching were no longer allowed. Well, he wouldn't be persecuting Jack like that. Far from moving out of the way, Bone stepped firmly in front of the graveyard gates and folded his arms across his chest, the sensitized skin of the blood ring around his heart prickling with fear.

Guisely looked uncertain for a moment, then squared his shoulders. 'Don't say much, do you, big man?'

Bone shook his head.

'Well, as you're not a parent or official guardian of the boy, I'm in loco parentis while he's meant to be at school,' said Guisely. 'So I think you'll find,' he added casually, staring at a spot beneath Bone's chin, 'that I can do whatever I want.'

And he moved to step around Bone.

It was the final straw. For years, decades – almost a century – Bone had withstood the taunts and reprobation, the downright fear and disgust of those who looked upon him. Everything about him they mocked. His odd appearance. His quietness. His obvious unrequited devotion to Lady Diselda Bootle-Cadogan. Scathing individuals like this sad little man had made his life a torment for as long as he could remember, and now the weasel was going to do the same to Jack.

Over my undead body, thought Bone.

And as the girl called out, 'Go on, sir – he's not that scary,' and Guisely held out a hand to push him aside, Bone took off his glasses, flashed his purple eyes at Guisely, then threw back his gleaming head. 'Siiiiiiirrrrr!' he yelled in a great bovine bellow that shook the gravestones, then he bent down to where Guisely had stumbled in terror, picked him up by one leg and slung his fear-stricken body back into his car. The girl watched the whole thing with wide black eyes, then as Bone stepped towards her she held up both hands. 'I'm going!' she squealed, and scrambled into the back seat behind the prone figure of her teacher, who was out cold.

Bone didn't want them causing more problems when Guisely came to. He slammed the doors shut, one after the other, and tugged the handles until they ripped off in his hands. Then he scrambled up the bonnet of the car until he was lying on the roof. From below he could hear the girl shouting, a great tirade of abuse that would have made him blush if he'd been able to.

Sorry, he thought, but you've chosen your fate.

Dangling his long arms across the roof, Bone grabbed the car's frame, and squeezed. With a great groaning of metal that set the jackals howling once more, the car caved in slowly, almost elegantly, until Bone found himself lying on top of a vehicle that was shaped like a number eight, squashed together into a neat waist in the middle with Guisely in one side and West in the other. They wouldn't be getting out of there in a hurry.

The girl glared ferociously at him through the back windscreen as he slid back to the ground, then pointed up at the sky. An enormous bird of prey circled overhead. Bone felt the familiar stab he experienced whenever an almost-memory occurred to him, but then a shout from the direction of the crypt reminded him of his more urgent mission.

Jack.

Under threat.

That was *not* to be tolerated.

Those boys were about to get a taste of their own bullying medicine. If fear was what they wanted, then fear they would have. But first a change of outfit was required.

Ignoring the enormous wingspan blocking his view, Bone hollered as loud as he was able, though the result was more like the honk of a enormous goose. 'Siiiiir!' Bone's coming, he wanted to say. Don't worry. Bone's coming. Bone is back.

Then he thundered into the crypt, knocking a boy with either fist so that they crashed against the walls, so unexpected was his attack. Having made sure they were too dazed to see what he was doing, Bone dived behind the altar.

25

Jack peeked over Vera Cornthwaite's gravestone at Moonshiner and Finch. They were running straight at him, little knowing that they were bumbling their way through a soupy fog of graveyard ghosts. Any second now they would find him.

Unless . . . unless he disappeared. With his new powers he could be somewhere else – anywhere else – in mere seconds. Yes! But while his powers tried desperately to comply, all he could envisage was where he was trapped. And then, worse still, he thought about the scuffling sounds of the boys' feet, the snorts and grunts emitting from the unfit Wormwood Moonshiner. 'Don't! Don't picture them!' he told himself.

Too late. Zzzzzzumph! He slid away from the gravestone, straight into Moonshiner's knees. Jack closed his eyes in quiet desperation. This was it. The end. His secret would be all over the school. Compared to him, the two goons cavorting around the graveyard would be the very essence of normality. It would be a mental institution for him, and possibly for his mother too, when she saw what her son had become. Mother. He pictured the expression on her face when the men in white coats came to lead him away. Mother, he thought . . .

And – *boommppph!* He was off, zipping along on his bottom back through the graveyard, crypt door, crypt, museum, whole west wing, Long Gallery . . . He couldn't stop. It was all too fast; Jack cried out as portraits whisked by him in a blur, the polished floors seeming to make him go even faster . . . Where was he going?

Just as suddenly as he worked out that he was headed towards his mother, he slid to a stop at her feet, tucked away under her desk. His heart nearly stopped with fright. Oddly, though, she had hardly moved. As he collapsed on to a neat brown shoe his mother pushed him away with her foot, continuing to talk above his head.

'No, no, we do understand, headmaster, and thank you so much. Roger, get off.'

Jack sniffed the air suspiciously. Roger? He nosed

his way forward, and this time she hoofed him right in the ribs. 'Roger! Away!'

Aha! She assumed *he* was Roger, her old and vile-smelling gun dog. He almost laughed out loud. 'Sorry, headmaster, these wretched dogs . . . I know. Yes, to-morrow at 10 a.m., and I hope we can persuade Jack to behave a little more like the lord he will one day become . . . We'd be delighted. Goodbye.' There was a pause as she replaced the old-fashioned telephone on its stand, and then a hand fumbled around under the desk.

'Roger! Who's a good boy? Yes, who's a good boy? Give Mumsy a kiss.'

Oh my life, thought Jack. Now that she thought he was her favourite hound, only one thing would stop her from getting down on her hands and knees beneath the desk . . . Trying not to retch, Jack reached out slowly with the tip of his tongue . . . and licked her hand.

His mother cackled with delight. 'Derj my beeby! Whooj my beeby? Yesh, Roger'j my beeby,' she warbled, tickling his ears.

Jack had to endure this torture for a further three minutes before his mother declared, 'This isn't getting

211

Jack into Eton,' and swept from the room. He got up slowly and stared at the website blinking from his mother's computer. For once it wasn't one dedicated to the planting patterns of the lesser-spotted begonia. It showed a building rather like Lowmount itself, and a strange picture of a bunch of dangling legs in stripy socks. 'Eton! No – don't look!' he hissed suddenly.

But it was too late. He'd seen it. He'd thought about it. He'd even said it. And now he was on his way. It took about thirty seconds, warp speed. Jack took one moment to stare at the building, so beautiful compared to Clearwell Comp, and so absolutely not for him, and then he pictured the library back at Lowmount. *Zum-mmph!* He was back.

This blasting around was tiring, mentally taxing more than anything. And he really wanted a dog biscuit. Picturing the boot room where the dogs' food was kept, Jack zipped through a few walls and floors and plopped down next to the real Roger, who growled half-heartedly with his chin on his paws, and then ignored him as he rifled through the cupboards. It was . . . well, handy . . . having hands, even if he did have a dog-head. He patted Roger, muttered, 'Whooj my beeby? Yej, Roger'j my beeby,' and then propelled himself back to the library with a bag of pigs' ears and charcoal biscuits.

Granny Dazzle had loved the library, and for the first time Jack could see why, even without the white-knuckle pleasure of the library-ladder ride. He could even smell why. The floor-to-ceiling books positively thrummed with memories, knowledge, information, stories . . . It was a place where silence was necessary because there was so much to listen to. The very emptiness was filled with history, with the breath of his ancestors.

'Right. Let's find out about this thing you and your ghostly pals want me to do, Granny D.,' said Jack after a while. 'Information,' he ordered, picturing a nondescript shelf filled with old, untitled books, 'on the Opening of the Mouth ceremony.'

Brooooomph! Before the last syllable was out of his mouth, Jack had shot through four different shelves and a library ladder, and found himself standing in 'Egyptology', positioned directly next to Granny Dazzle's quarters. Jack smiled. He should have realized. The section stretched for several shelves, and he was just beginning to wonder which book he should start with when his quivering black nose began to sniff out a scent.

It was wonderful. Lavender. Neroli oil. A slight whiff of something sharp, like ammonia. Cat litter trays. Definitely cat litter . . .

Jack followed his nose to the book that smelt of Granny Dazzle. It was not the encyclopedia he'd expected, but a slender volume the size of his French vocabulary book at school, with a hard back and a cloth spine. He peered at the writing, his vision blurry for the first time in his life. 'Well, you are a dog, Jack,' he muttered. 'Probably colour-blind now or something.' Hmm. Maybe those flags at the Comp hadn't been messed with. He just hadn't seen them properly . . .

Jack opened the cover to the flyleaf, and gasped. '"The search for Osiris, by Lord Jay Bootle-Cadogan. Dedicated to Diselda Carruthers – always in my heart." He wrote a book!'

Even if there was only one copy of it in the whole world, it made Jack immensely proud. Furthermore, he knew it would contain exactly the information he needed.

Jack spent a very happy few hours snuggled into a moth-eaten chair reading all about his great-grandfather's trip to the deserts of Syria. A lot of it he knew already (the legend of Osiris, for instance) and some of it was very boring (how many flannel shirts as opposed to cotton he should take, endless lists of all sorts of tedious facts and figures) and some of it he did not want to know (how much he was smitten by the beautiful Diselda Carruthers and admired her dimpled knees) but it made him feel he knew Grandpa Jay – and Granny Dazzle – far, far better.

The sun was just setting as he reached the part he needed.

My mouth is opened by Ptah,
My mouth's bonds are loosed by my city-god.
Thoth has come fully equipped with spells,
He looses the bonds of Seth from my mouth.
Atum has given me my hands,
They are placed as guardians.

From the Book of the Dead, these words would be spoken pre-burial by the priest to allow for the replenishment of the deceased through food or water or spiritual nourishment. From thence would the deceased pass to the underworld for testing by Anubis, God of the Dead. If they passed the Weighing of the Heart, they could transcend to the Field of Rushes.

Jack sat up. 'Hang on a minute,' he said, as much to his great-grandfather as to himself. 'Even if I am Anubis, it's too late for me to perform all that pre-burial stuff. Granny Dazzle and her friends have already been buried.' Without digging them all up, or finding the people who buried them all, there was no way he could find out what had happened to them before they were settled into the earth. Then he thought of something.

He did know who'd buried them all. He'd passed them when he was shimmied home from school earlier by his dog-god powers!

Less than two seconds later he arrived beside the bed of Will Waite, undertaker to the village. The sleeping man looked so peaceful. Jack didn't want to scare him to death, waking him to find a person with the head of a dog standing over him. Give him until daylight at least, he thought. Then he'd rouse the man with a couple of gentle barks.

Meanwhile there was time for a much-needed cat nap. No, not a cat nap – a dog doze. Jack snuggled down in the bedside chair, leaned his muzzle on the armrest, and nodded off.

26

So this was how Jack had been getting to and from the graveyard gates so quickly. Racing down the tunnel behind the altar after silently covering his tracks, Bone walloped through the door into the museum and sprinted to the corner display.

They were still there. Bone couldn't actually believe that Lady Diselda had kept his old bandages. They weren't even important. But as she'd once pointed out, they were the only piece of his history that Bone had arrived with, the only items he could genuinely call his own.

He stared for a moment longer, gazing intently at the strips of old cloth in the corner of the display cabinet, willing them to speak, to give him more information, fill in his past. But of course they lay silent. After a moment Bone raised his hand, applied the tiniest amount of pressure he could possibly manage, and promptly smashed the cabinet to smithereens.

He groaned wearily. He would clear it up later. But right now he needed to get on with the matter at hand.

As he planned his next step Bone cast a furtive glance around the museum. The Eye of Horus on the back of the door felt strangely intrusive, as if it was watching him. Bone smashed through that as well.

Now satisfied that no eyes were upon him – literally – Bone stripped off down to his neat underwear, averting his eyes from the crusty ring of blood on his pale shiny chest. After all these years, it still disturbed him that he could never erase it. Then he began painstakingly to cover his body from foot to head in his ancient, tattered bandages. If there was any glass from the smashed cabinet caught in the folds, he did not feel it, nor falter in his dressing. There was a job to be done. And Jack needed him.

'Siiiiiir,' vowed Bone, flipping open the jagged line of his mouth. 'Siiirrr!' he cried, more vehemently this time. Thanking his beloved Diselda for providing him with quick passage, he stumbled clumsily through the tunnel, not minding the dark, his purple eyes adjusting quickly to the gloom.

The crypt door. He roared, getting into character, excited at the prospect of ridding Jack of the nasty, verminous boys. The door flew apart with one strike of his overpowered fist, the pain barely registering as the sharp waft of candle flames pierced the air.

'Aaaaargh!' His enraged shouting nearly tumbled the roof of the crypt; it certainly grabbed the attention of the two boys – Snarky and Stupid, as Bone had decided to call them. They'd obviously been trying to set fire to the place, not realizing that stone is very difficult to light. The room was filled with acrid smoke, and the sight of the blackened walls along with the fact that there was no sign of Jack made Bone holler all the more.

The boy he called Stupid, the one with no neck, fell over in shock and lay there twitching, arms waving feebly in the air as Bone strode over and picked him up by the shoulder. Snarky didn't look so petrified, and Bone was sure he would have found something smart to say if Bone's bandaged hand hadn't clamped itself over the boy's mouth and lifted him clear off the floor. With a simple kick, Bone toppled the hefty door to the graveyard clean off its hinges, then he lumbered up to the gate with a boy in each extended arm.

Jack's odious teacher and the girl had managed to worm their way out of the mangled car and were trying to hot-wire the Daimler to make a quick escape, but at the sight of the mummified Bone clutching two of his pupils the man fainted again, slumped against the steering wheel with the horn blasting directly into his ear. The girl stared coldly from Bone to the boys and her teacher and back to Bone again. Then, with a quick shrug, she hauled Guisely off the Daimler's steering wheel and slid over into the driver's seat herself. Bone was almost impressed. The girl had spirit. Maybe Diselda would have liked her after all.

Without giving the boys a second to recover, he dropped them through the sunroof of the Daimler into the back seat. Jack's back seat. Peering down at them, he wagged a bandaged finger and growled, 'Ssssiiiiiirrrr,' one last time, just because he was enjoying himself now. Then he picked up the end of the car, spun it around so it faced down the road back towards the school, and gave it the most enormous shove with his super-sized hands. It hurtled back through the village as if jet-propelled. Knowing the

Daimler as he did, Bone was pretty sure it would hit a hillock and lie inert until the next shove. Well, let those nasty creatures stew in it until he – HE – decided it was time for them to move on.

Bone allowed himself a small grunt of satisfaction, which erupted from him like the mating call of a herd of camels, and then he headed back into the crypt in search of Jack.

27

In the morning Wee Willie Winkie Waite poured out two cups of tea, then, after a moment's thought, tipped one into a pudding bowl and handed it with a shaking hand to Jack. 'I've always known you'd come. The monster of the undead, the animal-headed demon god . . . just as we were warned.'

Jack blew on his tea, finding it rather hard to purse his lips with a long muzzle. No wonder he'd never heard of a dog whistling.

'I'm not a monster, I'm . . .' What was he though? He could see the man trying not to stare at his canine features, and the strangely familiar outfit he was wearing beneath his blue-black head. Probably quite monsterish. This was not the time to reveal his schoolboy identity and tell the man he'd actually known him all his life. 'OK, fine,' he said. 'I'm a monster. But why have you been waiting?'

'Because of the letter my mother received from

Albie – my brother,' Will added hastily. 'She never showed it to me, but she insisted from the moment she received it that we do everything in it. Everything, she said, to the absolute last detail. She was especially adamant that we should be ready for the monster coming, and there was something about a demon with a mismatched head and body.'

Jack thought quickly. 'Where's the . . .' He didn't sound very monster-like, or look it, lapping up Lapsong Souchong with his tongue. 'The letter is where?' he boomed in a voice that would have impressed even Mr Guisely.

Will Waite jumped out of his seat, then sat down again quickly. 'It . . . it's . . . She never let it out of her sight, even in death. She took it to the grave, as Albie made her promise.'

'Aha!' Jack paced over to the window, watching the sun set over the Hall. It was a nice view, one he didn't normally get to see. Focus, Jack, he thought, before he found himself zipping home in a rush. 'That's what I wanted to talk to you about. When she was buried,' he said, 'did you do anything special to her body?'

The old man rubbed his tufty chin, glancing almost enviously at Jack's abundant locks. 'No. Well, only what we have done with everyone, since Albie's instructions.'

'And what's that?'

For a moment Will Waite looked afraid. 'You will not harm me, m-master . . . if we have not done your bidding quite as you would have wished?'

Jack nearly laughed, but instead he said, 'No,' in his new gruff voice, and then intoned darkly: 'I . . . pinky . . . promise.'

'Well then, I believe the letter said . . . that the Egyptian gods had been angered by what Lord Jay and my brother had done, finding and exposing the grave of Osiris.' Will Waite stared into his teacup, unwilling to meet Jack's eye. 'They were warned of the curse that an . . . ahem . . . a demonic animal mutation would pursue them to the end of time, and make them serve him always.' He cringed a little, his cup rattling on its saucer.

'Oh. That's not me, you know. You don't have to serve me.' What was it with everyone thinking he wanted servants? Jack sat down again to put Will Waite at ease, tucking his trainers carefully beneath the seat.

A little encouraged, Will continued in his crumbly voice, pausing only to mop his beaded forehead with a large maroon handkerchief. 'Albie grew up in the family business, so he knew a bit about embalming and so on. He said – insisted, it seems, in this letter – that any burials we organized here must be done to Ancient Egyptian specifications, especially any for the Bootle-Cadogan family, or our own.'

'So . . . Ancient Egyptian specifications. What does that mean exactly?' He could only think of one thing Egyptians were famous for . . .

Will Waite nodded. 'Mummification.'

'You mummified Granny Dazzle?' squeaked Jack. 'I . . . I mean, Lady Diselda?'

'Not the good lady – but everyone else,' said Will.

'Right,' said Jack. 'I've seen quite a few dead people floating around.'

Suppressing a shudder, Will explained: 'Just to be sure, we mummified anyone who died locally from the moment we received that letter. We carried out the Opening of the Mouth ceremony for them all, with Lady Diselda in attendance – because of Lord Jay's involvement, she was the only person besides us who knew the ritual. And we took payment from the Bootle-Cadogan family in the old-fashioned currency . . .'

'Sheep and goats, instead of debens,' said Jack with a nod. It was starting to make a strange kind of sense. All the ghosts he'd been seeing were of people who had been mummified, buried in the Ancient Egyptian way with the Opening of the Mouth ceremony performed . . . and assisted by Granny Dazzle! No wonder she'd had a hidden tunnel to the crypt. And kept pretending she was off dancing. 'Hang on a second though. I thought that's what they all still needed – this Opening of the Mouth thingy,' he said, forgetting he had a long face and smacking himself in the chin as he pointed to his own mouth, mimicking the figures he'd seen.

Will shook his head. 'The ghosts must be doing it on Lady Diselda's behalf – she hasn't yet received the Opening of the Mouth ceremony because by then she wasn't around to assist.' He cowered in the armchair, one arm across his face as if fearing Jack would strike him down with one big lick of his doggy tongue. 'Did we serve you well?'

'Um, yes, very good.' Jack sighed. 'And I'll help you with Lady Diselda.' It was obviously what all the ghostly fuss was about. He was going to have to help ransack his great-granny's grave and Open her Mouth. Ick.

'Oh, sir, how kind you are! You are not great and terrible at all. Then she can pass into the underworld for the Weighing of the Heart by the mighty Anubis . . . Oh!' Will peeked over his arm at Jack, taking in his black dog-head and then letting his eyes trail down over Jack's dishevelled appearance. 'The mighty –' and he paused as if to suggest that now he was over the shock there was nothing terribly mighty about it – 'Anubis is . . . is you?'

'Apparently,' said Jack with a sigh.

Suddenly Will looked up at the window and then back at Jack, his respect renewed, terror etched across his face. 'They come to find you, m-m-master,' he whispered hoarsely, pointing to the window behind Jack with his right hand and then grabbing his own left arm. Jack stared at the grey face of the undertaker and followed the man's terrified, fluttering eyes.

The sight that greeted him when he turned around was extraordinary. First of all the Daimler hurtled backwards down the lane past the cottage, the bewildered faces of Finch, Moonshiner and Minty West gurning through the windows and Mr Guisely trying to climb out of the sunroof. They shot out of sight, and then an amazing creature lurched up the road after them, shaking his fist and bellowing after them like an injured moose. 'Siii-iiirrr!' screamed the bandaged figure, shuffling forward to make sure the Daimler had disappeared, which indeed it had, ploughing through a nearby field on a direct route to the school gates.

'One of them . . . has . . . escaped! Or is it the . . . the . . .' gasped Will Waite hoarsely. Then he dropped into his chair, both eyes rolling back in his head and a hand scrabbling at his chest.

'No! No no no . . .' barked Jack. Some Anubis instinct leaped up in his chest and the man's plight became only too clear – the sweaty brow, the clutched arm, the heaving chest . . . 'Don't die. No heart attacks! I know you're a hundred years old or whatever, but don't go and die now! It's just . . .' He looked back at the mummified figure, wearing tinted glasses over the gap in his facial bandages, marauding through the cottage garden in search of shade from the rising sun. 'It's just Bone.'

But it did look very much as if Will Waite had just dropped dead. Time of death: 8.18 a.m. Jack quivered between the clock and the body and then the window. He was due at Eton in an hour and a half, and travelling by Daimler was going to take an hour, even after they'd recovered it from the school. And he'd just killed Will Waite, the only person who knew how to mummify a body and perform the Opening of the Mouth . . . if that was important. It seemed as if it might be.

But all at once Jack was struck by the full significance of this strange transformation he was undergoing. It seemed that because of this family curse, he was the God of the Dead. He took care of the passage to the afterlife, prising mouths open and juggling hearts. If anyone could help Granny Dazzle and all those other poor ghosts, and the newly dead Will Waite, then it was him, Jack Algernon Bootle-Cadogan. Doghead.

He didn't know if his super-travel would work with luggage, but he wasn't prepared to leave the old man behind. Picking up the body as easily as if it was an inflatable bed, Jack pictured Bone in the garden. *Zjumpf*. He was there.

Bone stared at him from behind his tinted glasses, and Jack knew from his expression that his transformation must be more or less complete. He was taller too, on a level with Bone's eyes, the hems of his trousers flapping at his shins. And strong? Strong wasn't in it. He could have hurled Will Waite like a javelin and slung him into the next county.

Instead he said, 'Bone, we've got work to do. Mr Waite just died. I'm going to take him to the crypt and keep him in there tonight. We'll meet here later. Apparently we've got to hoick Granny Dazzle out of her tomb and perform some ceremony on her. In the meantime –' he pointed his whiskery muzzle down the road – 'you'd better get the car back and put your uniform on. Keep up the day job.'

Bone cocked his head on one side, his horrific yellow teeth appearing in a hole in his face. The man was smiling, Jack realized. For some reason Bone liked what he saw. Or perhaps what he heard. The man reached out a bandaged hand and gently stroked the top of Will Waite's head, a mewling sound bubbling in the back of his throat, and then he snapped open his jaw, muttered, 'Sir,' with a nod in Jack's direction, and plunged off into the undergrowth, shedding bandages as he ran.

'Crypt,' said Jack, allowing the picture to fill his mind's eye completely.

He'd always felt at home there. Maybe now he knew why. Death was second nature to him. *Zzoooop*. He laid Will Waite's body on top of Granny Dazzle's tomb, whispered, 'Back soon,' to anyone who might be listening, and then imagined his great-grandmother's museum. There had to be all sorts stashed in there, including a couple of Egyptian gods who could help him and Bone with the tasks that lay ahead.

28

The moment Bone had seen Jack materialize through a stone wall with the poor dangling body of Wee Willie Winkie Waite the undertaker in his arms and his majestically black canine head held high, he had understood. Somewhere in his ill-fitting memory banks, where pieces of information jiggled and bumped each other for lack of anything substantial to keep them in place, his knowledge of Ancient Egyptian lore occasionally took pole position. Here was what he knew: Jack was the Egyptian God of the Dead, temporarily at least. He had work to do, and he needed Bone's help. Will Waite was dead, and that was sad — so sad that it hurt; the last of the Waites gone, the last of those who had been connected with him and his darling Diselda. But between them they could move Will's spirit on. Bone and Jack were a team.

It was that simple. Bone allowed himself a little

exultant cackle and a click-your-heels-in-mid-air moment as he rounded the corner of the field in front of his cottage. As suddenly as it had burst out of him the laughter died in his throat. Even from this distance, and from behind tinted lenses, he could see that his cottage – his neat, beloved, well-cared-for cottage – had been completely ransacked.

His curtains were hanging in tatters through the shattered windows. There was not much, but what personal belongings Bone did possess were scattered about his rose garden in a random pattern, as though whoever had taken off with them had not been able to carry them all at once. His little bronze hand mirror glinted from the grass. Crooning softly, Bone hurried over to it.

As he loped across the field his vision suddenly turned black. He screamed as something attacked his bald head, wrenching the glasses from his eyes so the evening sunshine blasted straight into them, searing, ravaging, burning . . . then suddenly there were needles in his scalp, or daggers, a dozen knives slicing through his delicate skin. Blinded and staggering with the pain, Bone flung up one hand and batted whatever was attacking him back into the sky. There was a squawked cry, human almost, and then a flapping sound from over his head.

Bone fell to his knees and felt around for his glasses, blood streaming over his head and his face. He could picture himself: a steamed pudding, scarlet jam trickling down the sides of the pale sponge – just like Mother used to make. A furious squawk brought him back to reality. Locating his glasses, he shoved them on and dared to look up.

Far above his head an aerial battle was going on. An . . . eagle? Bone wasn't sure, but some kind of massive bird of prey, complete with the little leather hood they wore in captivity, was wheeling around the skies, legs extended, slashing madly at a smaller bird with sleek brown feathers and sharp, glinting eyes.

Bone ducked as the taloned twosome locked in combat above his head, then tumbled out of the skies towards him. Way above them, a tiny green rectangle floated in the clouds. What *was* that? Bone tried to focus. Suddenly, about two metres from him, the smaller bird broke free and raced, screeching, into the trees. For a moment the eagle hovered, the breeze from its wing tips stroking Bone's head, cooling the trails of blood against his scalp. The eagle fixed its gaze on Bone, and a chill descended all over him as his eyes met those beneath the bird's mask. Piggy. Small and piggy and nasty.

Gore and sweat dripping down his face, Bone pelted for the cottage, beating down the broken door with one thump and throwing on his second-best uniform. In moments he was off down the lane again, locating the Daimler, which he was not surprised to find empty in a ditch in the lane approaching the school. With one wrench of his hands it was back on the road. Bone leaped into the driver's seat and roared off towards the Hall.

He had to get there quickly. Jack wasn't the only thing that had been turned into a half-human, half-animal mutation. There were other forces at work here. Dark, unfathomable forces.

Because the freakish bird that had circled around his head hadn't just squawked at him . . . It had spoken.

Just one word, but drawn out, venomous and absolutely unmistakable.

'Die!'

29

Jack scanned the museum. 'Ozzy'n'Ice – you here?'

They were not. And time was pressing. Eager as he was to get back to the crypt and start embalming his great-grandmother, he knew what his mother was planning for the day. He'd have to get out of it, or . . .

Grabbing Lord Jay's ancient flying outfit, which he had worn to learn to fly as the First World War loomed, Jack pictured his bedroom and zipped along the corridors, very glad that Clare from National Heritage appeared to have no knowledge of his presence on the Long Gallery as he glided past her at express speed.

Once he was safely installed inside his room, Jack finally dared to look at himself in the full-length mirror inside the wardrobe door. 'Oh. No.'

He looked ridiculous. His head had become so hairy and stretched and pointy-toothed as to be positively wolf-like. The strange, blue-black mottled skin now extended down towards his shoulders and beneath the collar of his shirt. And there was more of it. More of *him*. He'd always been tall, but now he had to crouch to see his head in the mirror. His sleeves and trouser legs both finished three-quarters of the way along his limbs, and his shoulders had burst out through his shirt so that his collar hung around his neck like the choker necklaces Granny Dazzle had been so fond of.

Just as he was inspecting the inside of his mouth (the teeth were definitely quite impressive), there was a sharp rap at the door. 'Jack! What is going on?'

Jack skidded to the door and leaned on it. 'Morning, Mother! What do you mean?'

'Is Bone there?' The door handle rattled as his mother tried to come into the room. 'He didn't appear at breakfast, and Clare reported seeing him twenty minutes ago looking like some zombie character from a horror movie. More so than usual, I mean. We're due to meet with the head at Eton in one hour. One hour! Are you even dressed?' She shook the handle again, but Jack gripped it on the other side and it didn't so much as twitch.

'I . . . well . . .'

Dressed. It was a good question. How was he going

to manage to get dressed for this occasion? Or ever again, come to that? He changed tack.

'Mother, I don't think Eton's for me. Can we just give it a miss?' he wheedled, coughing as his voice got higher and turned into an actual doggy whine.

'Jack, I do not like the look of the company you're keeping at school. Those boys yesterday looked like ruffians. Ruffians! It's Eton or some form of correctional institution, as far as I can see. You've got five minutes. Five. Do you understand me, Jack Algernon Bootle-Cadogan?'

Jack sighed. 'Yes, Mum. Oh, I can hear Bone with the car!' He actually *could* hear Bone with the car, although with his canine hearing he wasn't sure if he was a mile away or fifteen. 'I'll get . . . grrr . . . ready, and see you out there.' This was bad. All his 'r' sounds were starting to form in the back of his throat. He quickly coughed again.

His mother's retreating footsteps slowed and he heard her mutter, 'Did he just *growl* at me? Oh, this Eton meeting had better go well.' Yet another thing he wouldn't normally have been able to hear. Being part dog definitely had its uses.

Jack waited until he was sure that the Daimler had

pulled up on the gravel in front of the main entrance. From the sound of two doors slamming and Bone's distant croaking, both his parents were installed in the back seat. Now, what to do about his tattered clothing . . .

'Crikey, Lord Jay, you must have been enormous,' he muttered minutes later as he pulled on leather trousers and jerkin over the shredded remains of his shirt, added long leather boots, and topped it all off with a vast white trench coat. He caught sight of himself in the glass-fronted cabinet. 'And I'm Scooby-Doo in a coat.'

There was nothing else for it. On went the flying helmet. Unfortunately it only covered his ears and the top of his head; his muzzle and great sagging tongue still poked out of the front like a wedge of sweaty black cheese. He zapped back to the museum. Foraging around in the displays, he found a gas mask from the Second World War and snapped it on over his face. Huge flying goggles finished off the outfit. His nose was squashed painfully into the end of the gas mask, and the whole ensemble was so sweltering that he had to stick his tongue out of the side of the mask, but at least none of him was visible. With one last horrified stare at his reflection, Jack took a deep breath and pictured the entrance hall.

Ping! There he was, looking out at the Daimler. Bone was bolt upright in the driver's seat, with a crown of sticking plasters criss-crossing his head, and his parents were both staring moodily out of their respective windows. Jack danced across the foyer to get Bone's attention, then mimed pressing a button. To his relief – at least one thing was going right – Bone spotted him without crying out in alarm, then smacked the button that raised the tinted glass between the front and back seats of the car. Scuttling forward in a crouch, Jack ran to the car and jumped into the front passenger seat.

'Let's go then,' he shouted cheerfully.

There was a pause while his father decided whether to reprimand him, and then he snapped, 'Forty minutes, Bone. Put your foot down.'

Jack would have grinned if his face hadn't been so contorted. His father was obviously looking forward to this about as much as he was. He pulled his mask down and stared at Bone, who glanced sideways at him with the merest hint of a shudder.

'Never mind me, look at you!' hissed Jack. 'What happened to your head?'

Narrowly avoiding smashing into a car on the inside lane and then into the central barrier, Bone mimed being attacked from the air, flapping a hand about over his head and then jamming his fingernails into his scalp.

'What?' said Jack. 'A hawk?'

Bone shook his head and spread his arms wide, as the Daimler careered about the motorway again to an accompaniment of shouted expletives and glass-rapping from the back of the car. 'Bigger than a hawk. Vulture? They like death. No. OK – an eagle?'

Probably, Bone mimed back, swerving from one lane to the next. Jack was just about to probe him further, remembering what Ozzy had said about Seth's ba, when his mother banged on the screen. 'I know we said we'd like to get there on time, but I would also like to get there alive!'

'Bone, what in the name of all that's sacred are you doing?' bellowed Lord Bootle-Cadogan. 'I said put your foot down, man, but do it in a straight line!'

'Ma'am!' croaked Bone. 'Sir.'

He looked distinctly uncomfortable. And suddenly

Jack thought he might be able to help. As long as his parents couldn't see . . .

'Eton,' he hissed, the building popping up in his mind's eye, and before he sounded the final 'n' he was off, scooting straight through the Daimler's burnished 4.5-litre V8 engine, out through the radiator and off down the hard shoulder of the motorway in a black-and-white blur. 'Not on my own!' he shouted. 'Back! Back to the car!'

Just in time he pictured the front seat where he'd been sitting, and suddenly popped up again next to Bone, whose jaw was hanging on his chest in astonishment.

'New trick,' explained Jack. 'Here, let me drive. Or at least hang on to the steering wheel.' He slid along until he was rammed up against Bone, then put his hands carefully at the ten-to-two position on the wheel. Years of watching Bone drive had taught him a lot. Then 'Eton,' he said slowly and carefully, picturing the building but also trying to build in an image of the car pulling up in front of it, complete with all its passengers.

And this time it worked. The whole car seemed to turn ghost-like; at high velocity it slid through trucks and sports cars and family saloons in the middle lane, causing a hair-ruffling breeze in the cars' interiors, before nosing through the stone support of a motorway bridge, veering off the road and whizzing in a shimmering black stripe to the outskirts of Windsor. They pulled up outside the school in the very spot that Jack had inadvertently visited the previous afternoon.

'Three minutes to ten!' he called to his parents. 'We made it! I . . . need to go to the toilet. Meet me outside the headmaster's office.'

'Jack? Wha . . . why . . . ?' gasped his mother, while his father spluttered like one of the estate's ornamental carp, 'What in the name of creation just happened?'

It was a very good job he didn't actually want to come to Eton, Jack realized as he jumped hurriedly from the car, ran into the hall and then conjured up an image of a headmaster's door. Arriving flustered and dressed like an idiot was probably not the best first impression he could make.

Knocking hastily, Jack propelled himself into the room and rammed the door shut behind him just as, in the distance, his mother's heels started to click along the tiled entrance hall.

The man behind the desk jumped in surprise. 'Can . . . Can I help you?'

Jack stuck out his hand and pumped the headmaster's hand energetically. 'Jack Bootle-Cadogan, sir, here for my interview.'

'And you're dressed like that because . . .' The headmaster looked him up and down, his eyes lingering on the gas mask.

'Because . . .' Hmm. He hadn't thought this one through. But then Jack saw the list of past headmasters on the plaque on the wall behind the man's head, and a glimmer of light shone through his fevered brain. 'Because this, sir, was what my great-grandfather Lord Jay Bootle-Cadogan wore, and he was an old boy of Eton. As was his son, Johnnie, and then my father, Jackson. It's family tradition, Mr Headmaster, and I take that very seriously.' He saluted, just for effect.

The headmaster smothered a smile. 'We like tradition too, young man. We also applaud the brave, and celebrate our differences, and I can see that you do too.' He nodded encouragingly. Then he checked his computer. 'But actually it's the lower master you need to see. Down the corridor, third door on the left.'

'Oh,' said Jack, backing towards the door.

'I'll take you myself,' said the headmaster suddenly, getting to his feet. Then he led Jack along to the correct room, where his parents were being seated in the corridor. His mother stared at him as though she might cry, while his father shook in his chair, muttering sideways, 'What in the name of Beelzebub is he wearing?' until the headmaster shook his hand.

'Jackson,' he said warmly. 'Always good to meet another old boy like myself.'

'Ye-yes.' Lord Bootle-Cadogan attempted a smile.

'You must be proud of young Jack here. He'll fit in very well.' As Jack's parents looked on, amazed, the headmaster clapped Jack on his newly broad shoulder. 'Pleasure to meet you, Jack.'

'Sir,' yelped Jack from behind his gas mask, where he stayed for the rest of a rather testing interview with the lower master.

Afterwards his heavy-breathing parents stomped out to the Daimler ahead of him, arguing bitterly. 'By all that's holy, you've gone and spent all your time arranging the flowers for that blessed open day tomorrow, like THAT's going to save Lowmount, and meanwhile our son's taking leave of what little sense he had in the first place,' sniped Lord Jackson.

His mother practically stamped her foot as she hissed, 'Well, you work out how to pay that ridiculous gas bill without declaring ourselves bankrupt. Our overdraft is like the national debt of a developing country, Jackson, and you don't seem to have any better suggestions!' As they slammed their respective doors Bone revved the engine to drown out the noise, and so began a slow, slow journey home.

It became even more tortuous when Jack remembered what day it was.

30

'Bone,' he hissed as they approached the Hall, 'it's the Clearwell Comp Comp.'

'Sir?'

'I have to win! Drop me at the back of the school.'

'Si-ir . . .' Bone looked as though he had rather a lot to say on the matter, but Jack didn't have time for a whole theatrical production of Bone-speak.

'I know. I'll watch out for eagles, and I'll see you at the crypt this evening straight after school to sort out Granny Dazzle. Oh, and Wee Willie Winkie. If I promise, will you drop me off? Please, Bone.'

Reluctantly Bone nodded. Jack checked the screen was up between themselves and his parents and stripped down to his ripped trousers and tattered shirt. He tore off what remained of the sleeves and fastened his collar carefully to hide the blue-black skin beneath, then sliced the legs of his boots away with his extra long fingernails so he looked as though he was wearing strange leathery trainers. He fished in his pocket for the little cotton square with his running number on it. Once he'd tucked it in beneath his gas mask, it covered any stray skin and fur. As Bone slowed the Daimler around a bend Jack opened the car door as silently as possible and tumbled out on to the grass verge. He lay there for a second or two, stunned, then quickly leaped to his feet. He was fine. Better than fine. He felt . . . unbeatable.

The starting line was a few hundred metres ahead. Guisely was stomping to and fro at the table with the entries on it, still looking a little dishevelled from his unexpected trip in the Daimler, while the competitors jostled and jumped behind the starting ribbon, and one lone teacher was laboriously ticking off names.

Jack smiled behind his mask. 'List,' he said quietly, zooming straight through a tree, out the other side, in and out of several other sycamores, and completely through the squat body of Mr Guisely, until he materialized in front of the tables. 'Jack Bootle-Cadogan,' he said quietly to the teacher marking everyone off; she barely looked up as she ticked his name. Then, as Guisely started to splutter in disbelief, Jack imagined himself on the starting line behind the others, and sliced through the playing fields to the edge of the woods to just the right spot.

Bang! The gunshot rang out, and the race started. Jack set off after the others, aware for the first time that he could see over all their heads, apart from the star basketball player, Fraser, and the thick dull hair of Minty West. Even Wormwood Moonshiner now only reached to his chin. 'How did you get in?' Jack asked, jogging to Moonshiner's side. 'I thought only the first three from each heat got through to the final. So that's Minty, me and Gouldian.'

Wormwood glanced at his mask suspiciously while looking around for his friend and trying to keep up with Jack, who eased ahead without any trouble at all. Gouldian was nowhere to be seen. Dropped out, maybe, which was presumably how Moonshiner, of the stumpy legs and T. rex arms, had managed to get a place. Jack looked left and right. He could relax. This was going to be easy . . .

But then suddenly he spotted a pair of hunched, pointy shoulder blades ahead of him. Finch! He was here after all! How had he managed to get so far ahead? Jack hadn't even seen him at the starting line.

Dooomph! He collided with the boy's back. 'Oh no!

Sorry, Gouldian,' he wheezed as he stumbled around a tree. 'Wasn't looking where I was going.' Stupid god powers . . .

But Finch didn't falter, or even look around to see who had pounded into him. Instead he sped up, following a fluttering scrap of material in the distance, white, like a little surrender flag. The route. Jack veered after him, and suddenly . . . *vvvrummmp* . . . there he was at the flag, ahead of Finch, ahead of everyone. 'Stop it!' he shouted to himself. Sure, he wanted to win, but not like this.

He spun around to see where Finch was, about to let him go past, get ahead again, but somehow Finch had not seen a streak of blue-black fur in a leather flying helmet shoot by him. His eyes were glazed as he plunged off to the left through the undergrowth. Jack watched for a moment, then took off after him.

'He doesn't smell,' he muttered. While normally that would be a good thing, Jack now found it quite alarming because Gouldian Finch always had quite a distinctive oily scent to Jack's sensitive dog-nose.

So whoever that was belting through the trees, it wasn't Gouldian Finch.

'Hey!' he shouted, hoping to stop the boy in his

tracks, but the bony knees just pumped up and down like pistons, driving the sharp-shouldered figure further into the woods. Jack sprinted after him, catching up and soon overtaking him.

He turned round, arms out, ready to stop the Finch-a-like, but to his astonishment the blank-faced figure didn't stop – it kept running towards him, and passed straight through Jack like an Arctic wind. And just as he gripped his chest to stop the strange pins-and-needles sensation Fake Finch had caused, four taloned feet clashed over his head, scrabbling for his eyes, while something black, shining and grotesque furrowed in a fast straight line towards him and attached itself to his feet.

They were all upon him – a hawk, screeching and flapping in outrage; an . . . eagle? Tremendous wings. Terrifying claws. One of them, he guessed, was the ba of Seth, choosing an isolated paddock to take him out completely – Anubis was Seth's worst enemy, after all. Jack swiped at them both, trying to shake off the hideous beetling creature that was attacking his legs, scrabbling up his body, making for his heart. Where had that thing come from? And where, oh where, were Ozzy and Ice when he needed them? Everyone was in this against him. It was a trap! And he was ensnared right in the middle of it . . .

But just as the eagle reached for his helmet and scraped it from his head so its talons brushed his ear painfully, Jack remembered the other competitors. He could hear them still, smell them, running over to his right. There was still a race going on. Like the race for his heart that was going on right there. And while there was a Clearwell Comp Comp, there was normality – kids who weren't gods, teachers who looked out for them, journalists who'd snap their photos for the local paper. There was still, perhaps, the slightest chance that even Jack could escape this madness, claim a bit of normality for himself. He had to win.

But the marauding birds of prey and the hideous beetle had delayed him completely. They were determined he wouldn't win. Wouldn't even escape alive. Well, they weren't the only ones with god powers. Gripping the grappling beetle by each of its massive mandibles, Jack cried, 'Finish line!' and tried his hardest to picture the white tape as the creatures closed in around him . . .

And suddenly he was there, with a nasty creature scuttling back into the undergrowth behind him, and an even nastier one staring down at him from the white tape.

'Posh Boy, this wasn't a fancy-dress race,' snarled Guisely. 'Fake dog-ears and a gas mask? You might think you've won, but you haven't.'

Jack gasped, 'Why? What do you mean?' as Finch, West and the Basketball Boy slid over the finish line just behind him.

Guisely bared his horrid nicotine-stained teeth. 'Not properly dressed. Not following the flags. And probably helped by your silly servants over there.'

Jack followed his finger. Sure enough, Ozzy and Ice were lurking under the trees, sitting on the magic camp bed like pensioners in deck chairs. It was all Guisely could do to contain his delight as he stood as tall as he could and announced: 'Posh Boy – this time you're definitely disqualified.'

31

Day job, Jack had said. Business as usual. How was that possible when Jack's world was disintegrating around him, and while darling, darling Diselda's soul was still in limbo, in peril?

Parking the Daimler haphazardly in the garage, Bone threw a bucket of water over it in place of the hours of careful cleaning he would usually devote to it, and switched off his pager. Lady Bootle-Cadogan would just have to manage her hordes of National Heritage ladies and the grand opening day without his help. Jack needed him for the big ceremony.

Inside the Hall, he stuck to the shadows and the less frequented corridors, making his way as stealthily as was possible for a man of six foot and three inches with stiff knee joints. To his relief, the current Lady B-C had decided not to open up Diselda's quarters to the public, and pushing open her bedroom door he went straight to the walk-in wardrobe.

Not really sure what he was looking for, Bone fought his way through racks of dresses and coats until he came upon the old portmanteau that had brought him back to her years ago. Opening the twin luggage compartments, he found that it had been given over to a very strange purpose. From one rail hung a couple of sets of robes, one for a man and one for a woman, judging by their size – simple, flowing garments in white, with a jewelled yoke that sat around the shoulders in blazing blues and greens. The bottom of the portmanteau contained shelves filled with little jars – bell-shaped, pottery, amber glass – all manner of containers for the precious oils within. In one corner was a scroll of parchment. Bone opened it up to find strange words scrawled in Diselda's familiar hand.

My mouth is opened by Ptah,
My mouth's bonds are loosed by my city-god.
Thoth has come fully equipped with spells,
He looses the bonds of Seth from my mouth.
Atum has given me my hands,
They are placed as guardians.
My mouth is given to me.
My mouth is opened by Ptah

With that chisel of metal
With which he opened the mouth of the gods.
I am Sekhmet-Wadjet who dwells in the west of heaven,
I am Sahyt among the souls of On.

What did it all mean? Sighing, Bone pocketed the scroll, then turned his attention to the rest of the portmanteau. The other side of the cabinet looked like something that might have been found in a garden shed: a peg-board was fitted to the back, and from it hung a number of instruments. There was a crook, like a shepherd's; what looked like the withered leg of a small cow; a long blade from which the head of a serpent protruded, the tip of its tongue forming the blunt point of the blade; a stick of wood resembling an elongated finger. Bone ran his own finger along the instruments and they rang out mysteriously, like wind chimes.

He had no real idea how these instruments would be used, but the instincts on which he'd had to rely for so, so long told him that these would be what was needed. Bone snapped the portmanteau shut and picked it up as easily as if it was a small handbag. Tucking it under his arm, he battled his way out of

Lady Diselda's clothing and headed for the museum, some ancient words beginning to march through his brain to the rhythm of the rattling instruments . . .

'In underworld, in afterlife . . .'

Yes, that fitted. Bone felt almost like singing.

'Eternal torment, endless strife . . .'

Well, those words fitted too. They weren't terribly nice though. Bone stopped for a moment, resting on the portmanteau. What was the rest of the song? The instruments within swung gently, chiming, ringing out the rhythm, and suddenly it all came back at once to Bone, as real as if someone in the museum ahead of him was screaming out the words.

'In underworld, in afterlife,
Eternal torment, endless strife,
Never more to be undone
Until two true hearts beat as one.'

Suddenly Bone's mouth went dry, as dry as he had ever known it.

He wasn't imagining it.

The song – the CURSE – was not in his head. Someone was screeching it out in that same infernal voice that had squawked 'DIE!' above his head. And it was coming from the region of the museum.

'Nooooooo!' moaned Bone. Jack would be on his way to the crypt by now. The . . . thing – whatever it was – was setting a trap for him. Bone would kill it. He would deal with it, before it could hurt Jack.

The museum was empty, objects littering the floor as at his cottage, and all at once another image penetrated Bone's memory. Tombs. Desecrated tombs. His purple eyes, well adjusted to the museum's murky interior, fell upon the card hand, the winning poker hand that Diselda had treasured because it had once been his. Two hearts. Two jack of hearts. With his enormous shovel of a hand, he opened the portmanteau and swept the detritus into the case, then folded it shut again and lurched down the tunnel, past the Eye of Horus, heading for the crypt and whatever monstrosity he might find there. It was only as he focused on the doorway to the crypt that Bone realized the enormity of what he was doing.

It was there again. The other monster that had screamed that foul word at him – DIE! Cursed him. Damned him forever. SETH! The evil green pig-head that had swirled in the doorway.

And now it was swirling again, right in front of him. It was too late to stop, and even if he'd wanted to Bone knew that he had to carry on, to get to Jack, to help Jack. Faint from the stench of noxious green gases, Bone careered headlong into the open mouth of the bellowing, fume-spitting pig-face, and felt once more the rib-cracking agony of his last meeting with Seth. His transformation began.

Bone was reincarnating.

32

'Ozzy'n'Ice, where have you been?' Jack ran straight past the crowd of bewildered race competitors to the pair beneath the tree. 'A hawk attacked me, and then an eagle and some kind of crazy beetle – would they happen to be those ba spirits you were on about? I think the Egyptian gods are out to get me!'

'We have been searching and protecting. You are right. From above we saw the eagle attack your man-servant, and the hawk attack the eagle. It is as feared – the curse has risen again with the death of Lady Diselda, owner of the protective locket,' said Ozzy solemnly. 'The evil one renews, and you must find him. You must destroy him.'

'Destroy him you must.' Ice stared unblinkingly with her startling blue eyes, then glanced down at the camp bed. 'Come. We will take you.'

Jack suddenly felt very hot. Annoyed – he was actually annoyed with them! It wasn't a sensation he was very used to, being pretty easy-going, but everyone seemed to want a piece of him. And he still had stuff of his own to attend to. 'I can't go now,' he said crossly. 'You go and find him, if you know where he is. You've got powers. I've got a dead undertaker to deal with, and my great-grandmother's ceremony, and . . . oh meatballs! What's he doing here?'

Jack stared, even more put out, as the Daimler pulled up to the edge of the field and revved its engines ostentatiously. 'Bone, what are you playing at?' hissed Jack. Tutting as loudly as his huge floppy tongue would allow, he turned his back on Ozzy and Ice, who were blinking rapidly at each other, and jogged across the paddock.

The window wound down.

'Bone, you know I hate—'

'It's not Bone, it's me, you fool. Get in,' interrupted the driver.

Jack jumped, not just out of fear, but so that his mutated head would be above eye level. 'Pops! I thought you were . . . You never picked me up from . . . I . . .'

'Yes, yes, I'm absolutely made of time – stand there dithering like an idiot, why don't you,' his father said with a sigh.

He leaned across to open the passenger door; Jack shot past it and jumped into the back. At least his father would have less chance of getting a look at him there. In fact, if he could raise the opaque glass screen between them, he'd be safe.

It was worth a shot. Just as his father sighed again and started to heave his aristocratic bulk around to talk to his son, Jack pictured the dashboard. *Zap*. He was in the front. With his father still staring at a space somewhere over his shoulder, Jack pinged the screen activator and then imagined himself sprawled on the back seat, and in the next millisecond he found himself exactly where he had been sitting before.

Lord Bootle-Cadogan watched open-mouthed as the glass screen slid up to the roof. Thankfully he was taking more notice of that than of his blue hairy son in the back of the car. The moment the screen was completely in place, Jack called, 'So was there something special, Pops?'

'Well, yes. Let me get this screen down first,' came the mumbled reply.

'No! Leave it! I mean . . .' Jack thought fast. 'Makes it far less awkward if we don't have to eyeball each other.'

After a moment Jack's father sniffed loudly. 'Suppose

you're right. It is slightly awkward. Your mother's sent me . . .'

Oh no. That didn't sound good. Mother Sending Father was only done in times of extreme difficulty. The last time had been when Granny Dazzle was about to die.

'She . . . she's not ill, is she?' said Jack quietly.

'No! Good god, no. She'd be a lot less trouble if she wasn't so damned healthy, if you ask me. No, it's . . .' Jack heard his father blow out his cheeks. 'She's had a phone call from the head at Eton. They were impressed, apparently. By you.' It sounded as though that was a complete surprise to Lord Bootle-Cadogan. 'They've offered you the Old Boy's Scholarship.'

'But . . . I don't want to go to Eton! I like it here.'

'Why, Jack? Do you have any friends?'

'Well, not really, but I'm . . .' Making some, he was going to say. But he wasn't, was he? Even Finch and Moonshiner, who were the closest he'd had to buddies, were turning out to be very odd indeed – zombified or . . . well, really thick.

Jack's father ploughed on. 'Are you achieving anything? How did you do in this cross-country shindig?'

263

'I . . . I was disqualified.'

'See?' cried Lord Bootle-Cadogan triumphantly. 'You don't fit in! You need to be with your own type, at Eton. Old money, Jack – that's us. Old money.'

'Old money?' yelled Jack, suddenly furious for the first time he could ever remember in his entire life. 'No money, more like! We haven't got any money, Pops. You can't pay the gas bill!'

The screen began to slither downwards. 'Now don't you take that tone with me, Jack Algernon Bootle-Cadogan. We've managed for hundreds of years. Some centuries are good, and some are bad. The nineteen hundreds – damned good for us. We're just going through . . . a bit of a bad patch, that's all.'

'No!' Jack didn't even care that the screen had almost disappeared into the seats, and that any second now the Lord of Lowmount would see his only son frothing at the edges of his doggy mouth. 'It's not a bad patch. It's the way it is. You can't go on living like Queen Victoria's still alive, Pops. And she's not coming back. You've got to get with the times!'

'Oh, like this Clearwell Comp,' spat his father angrily.

'Exactly!' said Jack. 'It's good for me. For us!'

'Not as good . . .' said his father, a very nasty threatening tone in his voice, '. . . as Eton. I'm enrolling you for September.'

'Fine!' screamed Jack, and he leaped out of the car.

It wasn't fine at all. It was so not fine that he wanted to attack something, tear it limb from limb and shake out the entrails. But as that wasn't really possible Jack settled for the next best thing. Pushing off with a bound, he set out around the village, running like he'd never run before. With super-human speed. With bounds that took him over fences like a prize-winning sheepdog. And with a feeling that perhaps, even for a rich kid who would one day be a lord, life wasn't always fair.

33

In the same moment that he was swallowed by the green pig-face at the entrance to the crypt tunnel, Bone was engulfed by the most potent rage he had ever experienced. Not again! This could not be happening to him again! This pig-faced evil god had subjected him to a lifetime of semi-mute, half-blind freakish-ness, which had cut him off from society, stopped him from reuniting with his beloved Diselda, prevented him from regaining his rightful position as lord and master of the Lowmount estate.

With a ferocity that astounded himself, Bone yelled and screamed and flailed his great sledgehammer fists around inside the vapours of the pig-head, crying out verses from a barely remembered script, not stopping to note that suddenly his frozen jaw was loosened and he could speak . . . speak . . . shout, even . . .

'O Fiery Eyes who came forth from Hermopolis, I have done no crookedness! O Bone Breaker, who came forth from Hermopolis, I have told no lies!' Told lies? He'd not been able to tell anyone anything for nearly a century! 'O Pale One, who came forth from Hermopolis, I have not babbled!' Oh, babbling! Babbling felt so good.

And suddenly the green mists around him parted, disgorging him with what felt like disgust on to the flagstone floor of the crypt. Bone leaped to his feet, stunned and dizzy, as the evil cloud-form swirled venomously over his head, then streamed towards the crypt's centre, arrow fast, towards the sarcophagus in the middle on which lay the dead body of Will Waite.

Bone ran, reaching out to hold Will's cold hand as the gases darted towards them. Bone's breath caught in his throat, turning quickly to a sob. The hands that stuck out from the cuffs of Bone's pale beige tweed jacket were young hands. Nimble hands, good with instruments.

Undertaker's hands.

That was what he'd been doing when the pig-headed god had interrupted him the first time around, all those decades ago. He'd been embalming someone – no, more than embalming. He had been protecting someone from a cursed afterlife by doing what would have been done in the time of the Ancient Egyptians. Protecting a friend by mummification, by removing his heart. A friend whose name began with the letter J.

Lord Jay.

'Jayyyyyy!' screamed Bone. 'I'm not . . . not . . .' Tears streamed from his eyes, steaming up his glasses, glasses that had reappeared when he encountered the demonic pig-head for the second time in his life, along with his old clothes, his old body. Or rather, his young body . . .

All these years he'd deluded himself. He wasn't Lord Jay at all. That much he could now see as he looked down at his too-big tweed suit, held the slender, boyish hands up to his face and then moved them over his trim moustache and thin hair. He didn't have the wonderful handlebar moustache. He was the other one – the young companion, the undertaker in training who had been invited to join the wonderful Lord Jay Bootle-Cadogan on his expedition to Syria and Egypt, who had been there when Lord Jay met Diselda Carruthers, and had looked on enviously, hoping that one day love such as theirs would be his, if he lived beyond his seventeen years.

He was Albie. Which meant that Will Waite was actually . . . his older brother.

'Will!' cried Bone in anguish, focusing properly just as the noxious vapours hovered menacingly over his brother's corpse, shimmered for moment, and then soaked through Will's clothes. The evil deity had entered the corpse of his poor dead brother, and Bone knew only too well what that meant. The body would be torn apart, cast aside as soon as Seth had no further use for it.

Bone was not about to let that happen.

The portmanteau was still wedged in the doorway, its contents scattered about the room. Some of these instruments would be useful. He tried to drag the trunk into the crypt, but it seemed that all his strength had left him. He was just an ordinary young man again.

And Will, infused with the venomous spirit, was levering himself upward in a sickeningly unnatural movement that had him snap to like a pocket knife, then sit bolt upright, staring out with sightless eyes across the crypt. Jumping down from the sarcophagus he stalked, stiff-legged, towards the door. Seth was on the move. He was attacking again.

Only he wasn't after Bone.

'Oh no. Jack!' whispered Bone.

Jack still needed him. And it was his lot in life to serve the Bootle-Cadogans, as it was theirs to serve Seth. Without another thought for his own well-being, Bone raced back for the portmanteau and began to heave it along the stone floor, after his brother's swaying cadaver.

34

After circumnavigating the village a couple of times, like an enormous greyhound on an even more enormous track, Jack began to calm down, his anger leaving him like the saliva dripping off his tongue. There were some positives to all this, after all. For instance, the back-of-the-car chat was the longest conversation he'd ever had with his father. The only one of the family who ever used to talk to him much was . . . 'Granny Dazzle! Oh.'

The most important task of the day – or night – had almost slipped his mind in the furore of the Eton interview and the Clearwell Comp Comp. But neither could really compete with interring dead Will Waite and Opening a Mouth for his great-gran.

It was already getting dark, and he was still in the vicinity of the school. Poor Bone would be waiting for him, all bewildered. Instead of taking off at a sprint again, Jack conjured up a snapshot of the front door to the crypt, behind VERA CORNTHWAITE, BELOVED WIFE, MOTHER, B-C CHAPEL ORGANIST, where Blackie had attacked him and he had first encountered the graveyard ghosts. No sooner had he filled in the details in his head than he was on the way there, travelling like a virtual mole through hillsides, brooks and country lanes.

He arrived seconds later at the ghostly location, which was bizarrely gloomy even for the time of day. True, it was a winter's afternoon, but this was a different kind of darkness – a green-tinged, foul-smelling fog like algae-thick pond water, with a soup-like density that clung to the fur on Jack's face as he looked around. Blackie and the other jackals slunk around the gravestones, sharp eyes fixed on Jack, waiting for his signal, for his command. 'Stay,' he said firmly, holding up his finger. To his amazement, the jackals flopped down as one, their gaze still following Jack's every move, until suddenly the amber lupine eyes shifted in unison, one metre to his left.

The crypt door was opening. Even without turning around, Jack knew that someone was stepping out and standing behind him. The fur on his neck was completely on end, and although not one had moved, the dogs around him were all growling, fangs bared. Slowly he turned around. 'Oh, it's only you,' he said with relief. 'Are you a ghost now?'

Will Waite turned, and Jack's heart froze. The man was still flesh and blood. Well, certainly flesh. Perhaps not so much blood, judging by the acid whiteness of the skin and the mad shrivelled look of the eyeballs that glowed through the gloom like burning coals.

Jack tried to stay calm. 'OK, so . . . do you need my help?' he asked slowly. 'To get to the . . . afterlife?'

The walking-dead body of Will Waite began to laugh, a dry rustle like autumn leaves. 'I have help already,' it said in a rasping voice that filled Jack with dread. Had he . . . had he been possessed? Will lifted a blood-drained hand and pointed to the skies. Even before he saw it, Jack's acute hearing told him what was coming: great wings and a vicious cawing. Then suddenly from the gate to the graveyard, zipping past the gravestones and out of reach of the snapping jackal's jaws, an enormous shiny black beetle raced towards the crypt entrance and leaped for Jack's throat.

Scrabbling spiny claws raked at his chest, tearing through what remained of his shirt, exposing the section of skin below his collarbone where blue-black merged into white. Instinctively Jack covered his heart and battled to push the evil, cat-sized beetle away. It looked like it was aiming to dig out his organs one by one, starting with the most important. As fast as he batted it away it came at him again. A blade sliced through his ear; yowling ferociously, Jack spun around to find Dead Will Waite slashing at him with a staff tipped with the head of a serpent, a gleam of mad glee in his horrid gimlet eyes. 'Blackie!' Jack roared as several sharp weapons attacked him at once, mandibles from below and Will Waite from just about everywhere else. 'Stop sitting! Stand! Get up, and . . . help!'

Luckily, assistance also came from all directions. Blackie and the nearest jackals leaped joyfully into the action, lunging for the humongous beetle with their snapping jaws. A small brown hawk dropped through the green clouds swirling overhead and went straight for the eagle that hovered quietly above. Behind them, two figures loomed up out of the gloom with eyes like headlights, one blue pair and one amber. Jack shouted in surprise as Ozzy and Ice swooped up to him, the whip aloft in Ozzy's hands, cracking through the air like gunshots, and his crook brandished like a javelin by Ice. Just in the nick of time, they attacked the serpent-bladed Will Waite from either side.

Momentarily Jack was left with nothing to do. The beetle seemed to be holding its own quite well against the pack of jackals, but now the dogs were getting advice from the ghosts, who were rising up from their graves, disturbed by the activity. 'Rip its legs off!' was what one teenage spirit was miming, while Percy the gardener was quite clearly recommending a good dousing with a ghostly sack of salt he had beside him. 'I thought that was slugs?' Jack yelled. Well, maybe it would work for gigantic beetles too.

Ice, meanwhile, had Dead Will Waite in a headlock with the curve of the crook. She pointed the serpent-headed blade into his face, while Ozzy lashed him into a makeshift net with the whip cord and was uttering strange incantations over his head, at the same moment as a light male voice drifted from the crypt doorway, chanting identical words . . .

'I open your mouth for you with the adze of Upuaut . . . Horus has split open the King's mouth, using that with which he split open his father's mouth, using that with which he split open Osiris's mouth, with the iron

275

that issued forth from Seth, with the adze of iron that split open the mouths of the gods.'

Just as Jack was about to step up and relieve Ice, Will hiccuped and belched horribly and his body slumped forward and fell against Jack. Time seemed to stand still as the worst nausea Jack had ever experienced, could ever have imagined, swept through him. He couldn't move. The sickness was in him. Every cell in his weirdly mutated body was infected by it, rotting and putrid and evil. *Get it out!* The evil spirit had entered him. Jack tipped back his dog-head and opened his mouth. The pain of a trillion needles was spreading through his body, and he was going to die, trapped in the head of a dog, so that nobody would ever know what had happened to him . . . nobody knew . . . except . . . except . . .

'Booooooooooone!'

As his valet's name burst from his lips, the evil that had penetrated his body spewed out of his mouth in a spurt of green gas. For a second or two it seemed to waver, an emerald spirit spinning in the air. Then it rocketed off into the trees and possessed the eagle. The huge bird immediately attacked the hawk and a ferocious air battle commenced.

Jack's legs buckled, as if the hideous thing that had possessed him had been all that was holding him upright, but then he realized he was also holding Will Waite's corpse in his arms. He leaned against the crypt door and straightened his knees to get a better grip, but just as he was telling himself how important it was not to let go, the crypt door opened and he fell backwards, dead Will Waite landing on top of him like a sandbag.

'Bring him here,' said a voice from the darkness of the crypt. 'I know what to do.'

Jack whipped his head around. He wasn't in danger, he knew that. The scent he had picked up was very familiar. But the sight that greeted him was not. Standing anxiously inside the crypt, holding what looked like the leg of a cow, was a boy. A young man, really, a few years older than himself and sporting a rather neatly impressive little moustache.

The stranger stepped forward to help him, remarkably unperturbed at the sight of a boy with the head of a dog crushed by the weight of a dead body. 'Who are you?' said Jack, levering Will's staring head off his chest. 'I recognize your smell.'

The older boy nodded. 'You called for me, sir. I can't explain it very well, but . . . well, I'm Bone.'

Jack helped the young man drag the body of Will Waite into the crypt 'Hey, I *know* who you are,' he said, suddenly remembering the photographs Granny Dazzle had pored over across the years. 'You're not Bone. You're Lord Jay's helper . . . Albert Cornthwaite.'

'Albie,' said the young man. 'That's what my friends and family call me.'

Jack gaped. 'But you've got to be about a hundred years old! How do you look so young? This is just *wrong.*'

'Says the boy with the head of a jackal,' snapped Albie. 'Look, I know it sounds like complete balderdash, but what Lord Jay and I did by uncovering a very significant Egyptian tomb provoked the wrath of Seth, and he killed Jay. I knew enough to mummify him so he'd get through to the afterlife, but in the middle of it Seth cursed us both: Jay to serve him – round up the dead, I suppose – and me to serve Jay with my very useful undertaking skills. Then he blew us up and we got squashed together in the sarcophagus, and my brain must have been damaged too. That's why I lost my memory and dragged my mutilated body home to Lowmount, unable to speak, taken in by your beloved Granny Dazzle who christened me "Bone", and why you're turning into Anubis – you're supposed to turn to the dark side and serve Seth for always, I imagine. No, I know,' he added, as Jack let out an aghast yelp, 'it's not how I would have had it, either, given a choice. Gosh,' he said suddenly. 'Perhaps that's why I was so drawn and hopelessly in love with Diselda. She was carrying a Bootle-Cadogan, a soon-to-be member of the family I had been cursed to serve.'

'Well, Bone, if that really is you, you're making up for lost time with the whole not-speaking thing. And, euw, you were in love with Granny Dazzle? Yuck.' Jack considered what Albie had said as he scratched his sore sliced ear. The young man was struggling to drag the body of Will Waite back on to the tomb, so Jack lifted the corpse easily into position and turned to Ozzy, who had followed them into the crypt. 'Is he telling the truth?'

Ozzy nodded. 'It is the truth.'

'The truth it is.' Ice smiled benignly at Albie.

'Lord Jay and Albie Cornthwaite found my final resting place,' explained Ozzy. 'Seth, my brother, was incensed, worried that this would allow me to rise up again and defeat him. So he cursed them both and destroyed the final piece of my body which would enable me to be whole once more. But my supporter Amentet managed to give the Carruthers Dancing Darling an amulet that staved off the curse until her death.'

'Till death it did stave,' beamed Ice.

'Her locket with the seeds in it!' Jack exclaimed. 'Granny Dazzle always called it her heart. She said some beggar woman had given it to her when she visited the site with Jay!'

'Not beggar woman,' said Ice. 'Goddess.'

So that was why everything had started to happen when Granny Dazzle died – Ozzy and Ice appearing, Seth awakening, jackals swarming all over the graveyard. Not to mention the small matter of Jack developing dog-and-god qualities. 'So I'm serving death from now on. Well, I don't much like it so far. And I certainly don't want to go all dark-lord and serve Seth. When we find this bit of you, this curse will be over? And my dog-head will disappear and all that . . .' Jack spun round to Albie. 'So have you got the last bit of Ozzy? He's missing a big chunk of his skull.'

'Ozzy? Are you meaning the great god Osiris?' Albie's moustache twitched nervously, as if he could barely bring himself to speak the name. 'And the sister-wife, Isis.'

'Um, yep,' said Jack. 'Ice'n'Ozzy, Ozzy'n'Ice, meet Albie the Cornthwaite.'

Albie bowed his head then spoke into his chest. 'My lords, I am afraid that I do not have the missing piece of Osiris that Seth scattered to the winds. I don't know where that might be.' As Ozzy and Ice sighed with a warm breeze that stirred the dust in the crypt, Albie continued: 'But Jack – Anubis – this I do know: the soul of my brother must be protected from eternal torment. We have to mummify poor Will, conduct the Opening of the Mouth ceremony, and then you have to pass him through to the Field of Rushes.'

'Oh, that's all then,' said Jack, barking out a short laugh.

Albie frowned. 'That wasn't a joke. I never joke.'

Jack could see that he meant it. Come to think of it, Bone had never been a laugh a minute either. Honest, caring, devoted even, but not exactly a comedian. 'OK,' he continued slowly. 'I know I've got some job to do, what with being the God of the Dead and all that, but I'm really not keen to start ripping into dead Will Waite and pulling his organs out through his ears or whatever.'

Albie glared at him with ill-disguised scorn. 'I can

281

do all that. Ideally we'd steep him in natron – that's salt – for forty days, but there's no time. But I'm a trained undertaker, and I know enough about the process to inter his organs in the canopic jars. We have your Granny Dazzle's equipment to help us. As for her, we've dealt with her organs – all that remains is the Opening of the Mouth.'

'So what do I have to do?' said Jack eventually.

Actually the Opening of the Mouth wasn't as bad as Jack had feared. Really it just involved chanting after Albie and waving a cow's leg around. They opened Granny Dazzle's coffin, Jack averting his eyes until he realized there was simply a mummy in there, and orated over her corpse. Then they danced around the sarcophagus lid a few times.

At Albie's signal Jack hoisted it back over his great-grandmother as if it was a cotton sheet. 'Why do you have to be a god to do this?'

'You don't,' said Albie, waving his arms, which were now encased in a ceremonial robe. 'You need to be a god for the next instalment, you might say.'

Albie waited politely for Ozzy to explain to Jack, but when the green god simply smiled, he spoke hesitantly. 'According to Egyptian lore, the heart contains a record of all the actions in a person's life. You must weigh Mr Waite's heart against the Feather of Ma'at, and if the heart is lighter the soul can pass through to . . . to Osiris. To you, sir.'

Ozzy nodded graciously.

'And if it's heavier?'

'It's fed to Ammut the Devourer and the soul is cast into eternal darkness.'

'Nice,' said Jack. He was going to have to dig out this poor man's heart and weigh it on scales he didn't have against some feather he'd never heard of, but even he knew what feathers weighed and he didn't fancy the odds. 'And I have to do this for everyone?'

All those ghostly graveyard dwellers were relying on him, and he couldn't see how to avoid consigning them all to eternal damnation.

'For as long as you are Anubis – I suppose so,' said Albie. There was a hint of sympathy in his voice, the echo of another soul in torment, trapped in a body that didn't work in this world – the body of Bone.

Jack paced around the tomb. 'But it's so not fair! I don't want to be a dog-headed god forever. I just want to . . . fit in!'

Disqualified from the Clearwell Comp Comp when he should have been doing victory laps and racking up new and normal friends. Eating the basketball. Having to befriend idiots like Gouldian Finch and the even more stupid Wormwood Moonshiner just to avoid looking like an utter loser and a loner to boot. Guisely, Minty, the wretched successful Eton interview . . . it was all for nothing. Normality was the furthest away that it had ever, ever been.

But there seemed to be no choice. 'All right,' said Jack into the awkward silence. 'Grab your scalpel then, Doctor Death. Let's get on with it.'

Would Will Waite bleed? Jack watched with one eye as Albie chose an instrument from Granny Dazzle's travelling case. How dead did a body have to be until it didn't spout blood any more? Wishing he'd paid more attention to *CSI*, Jack held his breath as the blade descended towards the corpse's side . . .

But no blood appeared. Instead, at that moment, the door burst open and the very people he'd just been thinking about tore into the room, every one of them screaming at him.

'What . . . what are you all doing here?' he said, bewildered, to Mr Guisely and the Clearwell Comp trio of school friends who ran in his wake.

Guisely took one look at the scene before him: Albie about to skewer the body of someone they'd possibly just murdered, flanked by three people with strange eyes and/or the head of a dog, and let out a scream that set the jackals off howling. 'What the—'

But Gouldian Finch shoved him rudely in the back. 'Do shut up, Guisely, there's a good chap. Beah-Ceah, delightful to see you. And you again,' he sneered, looking Albie up and down. 'A little reunion.'

Then his face turned green, and Jack found himself muzzle to snout with a loathsome pig-face that loomed oddly above Finch's narrow shoulders. 'You've been possessed, Finch,' he hissed, hoping that Gouldian could still hear him somewhere behind the mask of Seth. 'It tried to get me too. Fight it, Gouldian. Fight it!'

The pig-face gave a lopsided smile. 'Oh, believe me, I intend to,' said Finch, as the crypt filled with fumes.

Unnoticed in the corner, Mr Guisely uttered a feeble whimper and keeled over in a dead faint.

Somewhere in the fog, Ice began to weep.

35

'It is him . . . it is him,' sobbed Ice, her voice crystalline and broken.

Jack called out through the gaseous mists around him. 'Him it is, Ice, but don't worry! We'll sort him out once and for all this time. Albie, are you with me?'

It sounded very much as though Albie was not. From the tomb behind him came the distinct snuffles of someone trying to gulp back tears, and the kind of moan that only Bone could let loose was drifting around in the green gases. Vicious laughter echoed around the room from over their heads.

'Your friend is weak,' the vile voice snorted. 'Once before he tried to thwart me by removing the heart of the explorer. Now it is over. You will all die. End-lessly.'

As the horror of his words sank in Ice's sobs slowed to a faint breath in the far corner, near the altar. Some-thing thumped against the ceiling, and Jack realized why Ice hardly dared to breathe. Ozzy had gone after his evil brother. Some elemental godly battle was going on against the ceiling, Ozzy's skin merging with the green gas so that only a whirling emerald vortex was visible, spinning with sickly speed, pulsing and throbbing as the gods locked together in combat. 'It's OK, Ice. OK it is,' he called. 'Ozzy can look after himself.'

Jack prowled anxiously beneath the gods, his canine instincts guiding him past the crouched body of Minty West. What was she doing here? Waiting for her moment to jump on him, no doubt. She'd always hated him – although she was watching him now, and didn't seem at all phased by the sight of his doggy head. She cocked her head this way and that, eyes bright, listening . . . She was in on it, somehow.

His thoughts were interrupted by the sound of scuttling, and he recognized the scrape of the vast beetle's scratchy, vicious legs, the click of the mandibles.

Instinctively he jumped and found himself crouched on the end of Granny Dazzle's tomb. The beetle nosed him out and leaped for the stone plinth, gouging great wounds in Jack's legs as it tried to plunge its mandibles into his chest.

'Jack, duck!' cried a voice behind him, and he automatically dropped his dog-face to his chest as a serpent-headed blade swung above him, narrowly missing his pointed ears. The instrument caught the beetle in the neck and it crashed to the floor, spinning on its back. No sooner had it landed than a hooded eagle swooped down from the ceiling, the hideous snort of a pig coming from its beak. With a taloned foot it turned the beetle the right way up, and Jack bounded to the floor as the pair turned on him. Before it could reach him the eagle was plucked from the air by an enormous green hand; just as quickly it mutated back into a pig-head the size of the Daimler and tore back upwards, blood dripping from its slime-coated tusks.

'Albie, are you OK?' shouted Jack over his shoulder, sniffing madly through the gloom to try to establish what might attack him next. 'I can't see you.'

'Dogs are colour-blind,' called the older boy. 'It's all this green. But I can see quite well in the dark – years of practice and all that. Hard left – a bird!'

Jack swatted as a hooked beak screeched above his left shoulder, catching the bird of prey a massive blow to the head. It fell to the floor where the gases were at their thickest. 'It's the hawk. One down!' he called jubilantly, just as the pig-face pulsating above his head opened its jaws to laugh.

'Wrong one, Head of Dog,' sneered Seth. 'That was your own.'

'My own, Head of Pig?' Jack grappled with the beetle, grabbing it by a leg and tossing it like a frisbee across the crypt. 'What does that mean?'

The pig-head roared with delight. 'You do not know your own! Know your enemies, you people say, but knowing your friends is better still. I have mine. And that hawk was yours.'

Jack stared at the brown bird of prey at his feet. An ally? But hadn't it attacked him? There was no time to think about it as a fearsome green bolt of lightning struck from overhead, heading straight for the heart of the stunned bird. Making the most of his canine instincts Jack instantly stuck his foot out above the bird and took the full brunt of the fire-flash. Searing pain shot through his ankle and up his leg, and he slumped to the ground beside the hawk, which managed to open one eye just long enough to look gratefully at him. 'Who are you? Ice, is that you?'

Terrible, terrifying chants were whispering around the crypt, words floating down to him in dreadful soundbites that choked his heart, which even now was being sought out by the beetle. The hawk rallied slightly, tripping the beetle, then slouched back to the floor. Jack tried to move but the pain in his leg was too intense, and as he lay frozen on the floor of the crypt he realized that someone new had entered the fray.

Granny Dazzle was standing above him, pain in her eyes, and fear. And as other spirits spilled out of the walls to join her, to pitch into the battle against the enemy wraiths that circled the room, chanting their hideous incantations, Jack knew that he'd failed. Whatever it was that his great-grandmother had wanted him to do, he had not completed it.

'Granny Dazzle, I'm sorry!' he shouted, but his words were almost drowned out by the banshee wails of the green gaseous spirits, pouring out of the pig's mouth like maggots, sliding down the walls as they chanted . . .

'In underworld, in afterlife,
Eternal torment, endless strife,
Never more to be undone
Until two true hearts beat as one.'

Granny Dazzle's ghost glanced upwards fearfully. Then she looked to one side, even more afraid, and Jack saw the shimmering image of his great-grandfather staring at her sadly. Beyond sadly. Heartbroken. Now Granny Dazzle would never be reunited for all of happy eternity with Lord Jay, because he had not done his job properly. His job as a great-grandson, and his job as the God of the Dead, Anubis.

The attacks were coming on two fronts – the beetle raking through the fur on his scalp, the eagle-pig above posed to dive. It was pointless. It was over.

'*Until two true hearts beat as one*,' repeated Jack listlessly. 'Yeah, yeah. I get it. We're all going to die. Because two hearts can't beat . . .'

But suddenly, he did get it. Until two true hearts beat as one.

The deadly creatures were gaining ground, but he was a god. *A god!* He had powers!

Without further delay, Jack pictured the top of the tomb. *Zip.* There he was, next to Albie, who was madly brandishing the serpent blade at anything that came hear. 'What did you say the next part of this process is?' Jack whispered urgently.

291

'Weigh the heart against the Feather of Ma'at,' puffed Albie.

'Look, I know this is weird,' muttered Jack, 'but when Seth the pig-head attacked you last time, did you ... did you happen to have a spare heart on you?'

Albie frowned, thinking, and then he gasped. 'Good Lord!' he said. 'Yes.'

'Great,' said Jack, breaking off to kick the clambering beetle squarely in the chest. 'And do you happen to know where it might be?'

'Why?'

'It's just a theory,' said Jack, 'but a true heart would be lighter than this feather, wouldn't it? I know where one true heart is that I'm sure is lighter than this feather. If we can just find the other one, we'll have two true hearts. Granny Dazzle's and Lord Jay's.'

'Beating as one,' they said together.

'Hold them off,' said Jack. 'And try to think where Lord Jay's heart might be. I'm going to get Granny Dazzle's.'

36

Without another word, Jack zipped away in a streak of blue-back fur that quickly mingled with the odious vapours and disappeared. Albie stared for a moment at Will's bandaged body. If all else failed . . .

No. He couldn't countenance it. He wouldn't plunder his brother's body, although he was sure that William's heart would prove to be true. Hadn't Will been constant in his adherence to the instructions he had sent all those years ago? He didn't deserve to have his heart cut out, when there was every indication that it would be a pointless exercise, that they would all soon meet their dire, unceasing end in any case.

Cutting out Jay's heart had been different. Completely necessary. It had saved them. Oh, how it had saved them. Jay had been spared damnation. And he himself, Albert Cornthwaite, had lived, even though in reality this had meant that he suffered the living equivalent of hell: in love with someone he could never have, scarred and broken and feeble and yet apparently immortal.

He wasn't at all sure that Jack would achieve anything good from his plan, but it might just mean they could be saved. He had to give Jack time.

In Jack's absence the immense beetle transferred its attention to Albie, and he screamed with pain as it anchored its clawed feet in his thigh. The serpent-bladed adze slipped from his grasp, and the calf leg for the Opening of the Mouth ceremony was long gone, perhaps even eaten by the stray jackals outside. With a whispered, 'Apologies, brother,' Albie swung Dead Will's stiffened arm across his own body and knocked the beetle for six. It crashed into the floor a short distance from the stranded hawk, and Albie watched in surprise as the bird lifted its feathered head and pecked viciously at the beetle's back. From this height, Albie could see what it was. A scarab. An enormous, evil scarab beetle. Scarab amulets were often used in mummification to protect the heart, but this one was doing the opposite. Several times it had scratched at Jack's chest, and now it seemed intent on getting to Albie's heart.

He couldn't recall any scarab charms. The only one he could bring to mind from the Book of the Dead was meant for driving off a snake. In the absence of anything better, as the beetle shook off the hawk and made for his chest again, Albie flung himself off the tomb towards the tunnel doorway. The beetle took off after him, snapping its mandibles at his heels. Scrambling madly across the altar dais, Albie reached the portmanteau and grabbed the stick of wood resembling an elongated finger.

'O Rerek!' he screamed, pointing the finger at the skittering beetle. That wouldn't work. He knew it meant 'snake'. Sweating madly, beating aside the green writhing spirit wraiths that seemed to press against his skull, Albie jumped backwards into the portmanteau. 'O scarab!' he cried. 'Take yourself off, for Geb protects me. Get up, for you have eaten a mouse, which Re detests, and you have chewed the bones of a putrid cat.'

Although Albie doubted very much whether the beetle had ever gone after a cat, putrid or otherwise, the incantation seemed to have some effect. The beetle faltered, seeming confused, and just for a second Albie saw it elongate, grow tall, until it looked almost as though it was a boy standing before him – the boy he'd called Stupid – but then it shrank back inside its wing cases and scrabbled into the space between the trunk and the tunnel wall, trying to get at whatever was behind.

Jack must be heading back.

To give himself time to think, Albie pulled the doors of the portmanteau closed. What exactly *had* he done with Lord Jay's heart?

37

In less than a second Jack was in the museum.

'Well done, Granny D.,' he whispered. Although he'd never realized it, she'd left everything he would need right there for him to find. In fact, when the door to the crypt closed, and the fish-shaped eye that he now knew to be the eye of Horus scanned the room, he saw that it fell on all the right objects.

His scales. His by birthright, she'd said. He'd always thought it was because he was a Libran, born under the sign of the scales, but now he knew the truth.

Her feathered headdress. The one she'd worn on her wedding day, which had been a present from her fiancé. The feathers were not just splendid fluffy white heron tails as she'd led them to believe. Jack fingered the tips of the smooth fronds and was about to pull the biggest from the silk band that held them in place, when some instinct made him stop. The heart had to be lighter than the Feather of Ma'at. By now he knew for sure that the gods would not have made it an easy test, so they would not have been so obvious. Bypassing the biggest feathers, he plucked the smallest of the three from the end of the band, and knew by the way it thrummed against his hand that he'd chosen correctly.

'Right. Now for your heart.' For a moment Jack couldn't find it, and his own heart constricted. He wasn't going to be able to do this without her heart. But then, among the debris that Bone and the break-in had caused, an aroma snaked towards his sensitive black nostrils. Wood. A tinge of metal. Cat pee. The distinctive smell of Granny Dazzle. Following his nose, Jack dug around in the shattered remains of the musuem, and pulled out Granny Dazzle's necklace. It was the very same one she had strung around Lord Jay's neck when they first met. Her heart on a string.

With a wolfish grin Jack was just about to head back to the crypt when it occurred to him that Albie might have more trouble locating Lord Jay's heart than he had with Granny Dazzle's. 'Library,' he said, picturing the place where he'd left his great-grandfather's journal lying on the chair. *Zumph*. He was there. Jack tucked the little bound journal into his waistband, his heart thumping as he heard the unmistakable sound of his mother crying nearby. What was the room next door? Her office.

Suddenly her door opened and closed and a pair of heels clicked away down the corridor. 'Computer,' said Jack, and was instantly transported through five sets of library shelves and a brick wall into the next room.

His mother had been checking how many tickets had been sold for the next day. Despite all the wonderful website advertising, it seemed that there were more people in the crypt at present than would be coming along to the open day in the morning. While he was standing by the computer Jack suddenly thought of something. One of yours . . . the pig-headed god had said.

'Hawk.' He typed the word into the search engine, but got so many options he backed out immediately. 'OK . . . Nick Guisely.' Could he actually be a friend? It didn't look like it. Mr Guisely's name simply brought up a profile of Clearwell Comp and some unflattering comments on Friends Reunited.

Jack tapped quickly. '1149 British animals in danger,' read Jack after entering 'Wormwood Moonshiner'. '"This obscure beetle is endangered . . ." Beetle? Oh my life!' Jack pictured Wormwood stumbling around with no neck and stubby arms, and the image of an upright beetle became perfectly clear. Wormwood was just some kind of Seth creation. Seth . . . Gouldian . . . on to him from the outset, trying to get him alone, slyly attacking . . .

Jack did one last quick bit of typing and clicked on the first result. '"Also known as the rainbow finch, the *Gouldian finch* is becoming somewhat rare in the wild and is considered endangered." That creep! Well, he's endangered now.'

Finch. The name of a bird. What was it Ozzy and Ice had said? Seth's ba or spirit would appear in *the form of a human-headed bird*. A monster with a mismatched head and body!

Instantly Jack pictured the hooded eagle, piggy evil eyes glinting at him from the slits in the leather . . . and as fast as he imagined himself wrapping his hands around Finch – Seth's – scrawny evil neck, he found himself zapping through Lowmount Hall back to the crypt, straight into the very danger he'd been trying to avoid.

38

The pig transformed into the eagle before their eyes, dropping down from its prime attacking position above their heads. To Jack's horror, Ozzy was pinioned to the apex of the ceiling by an invisible sheath that seemed to be crushing him. Beside him, hanging upside down from the camp bed like a bat, Ice wailed and sobbed and tried to tear at the bonds with her hands, but whatever enchantment Seth had put on Ozzy reacted to every attempt to free him, constricting Ozzy further.

'Ice, leave it!' shouted Jack. 'You're making it worse!'

He'd found himself floating above the tomb, his body extended in the arc of a leaping dog. Now as his travelling powers recognized that he'd reached his destination, namely the eagle, Jack dropped like a stone, only just missing the corner of Granny Dazzle's sarcophagus as artefacts tumbled out of his pockets and bounced off in all directions. Streaking after him came the great bird of prey. Turning back on himself as if after a ball, like the dog that he was, Jack stretched out with his fangs and ripped the hood from the bird's head. Sure enough, and so vile as to make him want to vomit, the grinning human head of Gouldian Finch swivelled on the feathered neck, pig-eyes glinting emerald.

'Good Lord, Beah-Ceah,' it drawled in its phoney posh accent, meant to make Jack feel he could trust him. 'You took an awfully long time to work out the truth, what? So long you've just prolonged the agony. You should have let me finish you off at the race.'

But at the Clearwell Comp heats it had been Minty who stopped him, hadn't it? And the hawk and eagle attacks . . . What was her part in this?

Jack checked where his feet were about to land. Swerving neatly to his left, he avoided the still prone body of the hawk. It cawed thankfully, and for the first time Jack recognized the dark eyes. 'Minty . . . is that you?'

The hawk bobbed its head – yes – then rolled to one side as the eagle struck from above. 'Albie, what . . . ? Albie?' Jack cried out through the thickening gloom, about to lose sight of Minty the Hawk and completely unable to see the young Bone. There was a rapping sound from inside the portmanteau; sniffing his way across, Jack ran over and opened it up.

'Blasted beetle locked me in,' gasped Albie, crawling out. 'Turned into that boy with stumpy arms. Waved them about and moaned a lot. Reminded me of . . . well, me.'

'Feel free to kill it if you see it again,' said Jack. 'Swat it like a bug. Stamp on it like a cockroach.'

They broke off to stand back to back as the eagle dam-busted their heads then swirled up towards Ozzy, morphing back into its pig shape. Albie shook a long wooden finger at it and Jack gnashed his teeth in a way that Blackie would have been proud to.

'I'm glad you said that, Jack.' Alfie swatted at something near his feet, then began to jump up and down. 'Because it's back. And it's brought its friends. You do know a cockroach can live for six days without its head attached?'

'Great,' said Jack faintly.

Past the portmanteau poured a seething torrent of shining black cockroaches and stag beetles and all sorts of creatures that neither of them could put a name to, all with the same aim in mind, led by the mutated

Moonshiner in a mad stampede to scratch out some hearts.

'The Feather!' cried Jack, and he sprang over the tomb to the far side, where the feather had drifted. Minty the Hawk had beaten him to it, and was struggling to pick herself up off the floor with the Ma'at Feather in her beak. In one movement Jack scooped her up with his long muzzle and deposited both bird and extra feather on to the tomb. He leaped up after her. 'Albie, grab the scales and come up here.'

But the scales had fallen behind the portmanteau, and Albie was too terrified of the beetles to move, apart from some frenetic Irish-dancing manoeuvres to stamp them out. He inched closer to the scales, saw that they were full of shimmering beetles and pulled back. 'There's too many of them, Jack. Argh!' Several were heading up his trouser leg, and he shook them out frantically.

Jack couldn't help. Albie was right – there were too many beetles. They were massively outnumbered. Furthermore, they couldn't get to the scales, and without them they couldn't complete the next part of the ceremony and reunite Granny Dazzle and Lord

Jay, putting an end to this madness. If only they had more help . . .

Standing full stretch, he pointed his nose at the pig-head, which was still regurgitating wraiths and now the occasional asp, and howled. Outside, a chorus of howls responded. 'Blackie!' he yelled. 'In here, boy. Dinner!'

Instantly the door was knocked off its hinges as a pack of jackals hurled themselves as one into the crypt. Hundreds of beetles were squashed in one go; the rest scattered to the edges of the room, out of the door into the graveyard, or tried to get back down the museum tunnel as the dogs snapped and scratched and crunched whatever morsel they could catch. 'Ha!' shouted Jack. 'See how you like being eaten. Albie, come on.'

Using a couple of jackals as stepping stones, Albie jumped from the portmanteau, grabbing the scales as he went and shaking the beetles off it into the open jaws of a passing hound. In two bounds he was up on the tomb beside Jack, pointing the wooden finger at an asp dangling above Jack's ears. 'O Rerek, snake, take yourself off, for Geb protects me!' cried Albie, and the snake shrivelled up in a plume of black glittering smoke.

'Cool!' said Jack. He pointed to the hawk, who still lay dazed at his feet. 'And this hawk here tells me she's Minty West from school. I can't revive her though. Can you think of any names of Egyptian gods like that? Because Gouldian Finch is just the name of a bird, and he turned out to be Seth. And Wormwood Moonshiner is Beetle-Boy.'

'I-I can't think . . . err . . . Minty . . . Ammut? Ammut the Devourer?' stammered Albie, dropping the scales, whipping around to ward off the falling snakes and whirling spirits and increasing amounts of spit pouring from the fetid mouth of the pig-faced god. 'West. The west is very important to the Egyptians. The dead travelled to the west to find peace, on a boat across the river. That's why I kept imaging boats! Hah. Oh. And this crypt is in the west too,' he added helpfully.

Jack snapped an asp in half with his teeth, narrowly avoiding its fangs. 'So Minty could be something to do with death? But I'm the God of the Dead, aren't I?'

'Sort of. But . . . yes, there's a Goddess of the Dead too. And she carried a hawk on her head. Amentet.'

'Excellent, that's it! Time to see how good I am.' Jack dropped to his knees beside the hawk. 'Amentet of the West, Goddess of the Dead, I command you to rise.'

Where previously Granny Dazzle had spun, he cleared a space for Minty. The ghost of his great-grandmother was floating out of reach, stretching out her hands, beseeching, begging him to reunite her with her Jay, shimmering in all his mustachioed glory, before it was too late, but Jack could see it was nearly that time anyway. Her spirit was thinning, and the flames at her feet now devoured her up to the waist . . .

Before her stood Minty, still in her running outfit, a smaller hawk perched on top of her thick dark hair. 'Took your time, Dog-Boy,' she said gruffly. 'And this tomb is getting way too crowded.'

'Sorry,' said Jack. 'Um, this is Albie.'

'We were supposed to meet,' she said with a grin that made her face suddenly heart-shaped. Albie blushed. 'I was all ready to welcome you at the tomb of Osiris, but you cheated death.'

'And me!' roared a ferocious voice, snorting and spitting and throwing out all manner of evil from between tusks. 'But not this time.'

Jack looked up. The pig's mouth was getting bigger. Already it appeared to have swallowed up Ozzy, who could no longer be seen through the green gases. Ice too was vanishing in the noxious vapours. The back of the throat was aflame; any second now it would engulf them. They'd be swallowed whole, or maybe crunched like the beetles in a jackal's mouth, and that, he imagined, would be that. What a way to go!

'Quick!' he squeaked. 'Weigh the heart!'

As mutated creatures rained down on them from the ceiling Albie slid the scales across to Jack. Minty knelt and placed the Feather of Ma'at on one of the bronze pans, and the balance skewed up and down. Sliding the necklace back over his dog-head, Jack gripped Granny Dazzle's heart on a string between two fingers, took a deep breath and dropped it on to the other pan.

There was a brief moment of lurching up and down . . . then the side with the Feather dropped down to the stone top of Granny Dazzle's sarcophagus with a clang. 'Yay!' yelled Jack. 'Granny's heart is true!'

Not that he'd ever doubted it.

But it wasn't enough. Seth's evil pig-head above them cranked its jaws ever wider, a waterfall of inhuman creatures cascading down on their heads, making the tomb slippy. 'Two true hearts beat as one,' repeated Jack, unable to avoid the shrieking of the spinning, snake-like spirits heading ever closer. 'It has to be two. Albie, give me Lord Jay's heart.'

He held out his hand expectantly, sure that Albie was going to pass it to him, that Bone would always have kept it safely somewhere.

But to his dismay Albie shook his head. 'I don't know where it is.'

'But . . . you had it, didn't you? When Seth attacked before,' Jack whispered, hoping that would be a defence against the sensitive hearing of the pig-god.

Albie winced, craning his head back in a way that Jack recognized as Bone's normal stance. 'Yes. I had it then. But I . . . I think I posted it.'

39

Two hearts beating as one. Well, one wasn't beating exactly. But they had been in the same place, operating as one to all intents and purposes.

Albie suddenly recalled most of it as clearly as if it had been the previous day. The thick letter to his mother had been ready in his pocket. He just wanted to add a postscript telling her when to expect him home, so he hadn't sealed it. The rest of the letter was brutally clear. They had upset the gods. They would be chased, tracked down, and the monster they had called up would head to Lowmount. Most likely he would try to kill Diselda, pregnant as she was with Lord Jay's descendent. Jay – the first of the boys to be called Jack Al – followed by John (known as Jack) Albert, Jackson Aloysius and latterly Jack Algernon Bootle-Cadogan. Jackal B-C.

The Cornthwaites must protect the village and the estate. If they failed, Seth would turn them all into the undead and make them his servants. Once he had conquered Lowmount, his evil could spread in concentric cirles like a pebble dropped in a pond. The world was at risk. As undertakers they must embalm and mummify anyone in the village who died, to prepare them for safe passage to the underworld, in exactly the same way as he now did with the body of his friend and mentor. The letter to Diselda from Jay explaining her part in it was safely installed in the same pocket, so they could expect help from the Hall.

They must change their name, and hope that one day he would make it home to them.

But then Seth had roared into the inner chamber, frightening young Albie almost beyond the end of his wits. The heart. All he could think of was the heart. Without it Jay could not be passed through to the underworld. And if he wasn't in the underworld, he wouldn't be there to serve Seth as the curse he laid upon them demanded.

With his scalpel he'd levered the heart from the chest of his friend and stowed it in the envelope in the breast pocket of his jacket. The blood drained through the parchment in a painful, crusting ring around Albie's own heart, a ring that he was never able to eradicate, a constant reminder that while he had saved his friend, his own cause was lost . . .

Only one body had made it to hospital. That much Diselda had told him. One body, with two letters and a heart on a string. And as long as that heart on a string was alongside Diselda's, and Jay's heart was not reconnected with his body, the curse was warded off.

Now they needed Jay's heart. The curse would end. Jack would be restored to normality. But from that day in the tomb Albie had never laid eyes on it again.

40

On top of the tomb, Albie stared at his feet while Minty gazed calmly at Jack. He supposed death wasn't new to her, being Goddess of it and all. She shrugged her broad shoulders. 'You might as well try,' she said eventually. 'Nothing to lose. Everything to gain. Come on – don't make me hurt you.'

'What can I do?' Jack shook his head, aware of its heaviness. 'Albie doesn't have the heart, do you, Albie?'

'I've no idea where it went.'

'Well, when did you have it last?' It was the way Granny Dazzle had found countless lost objects for him.

'I put it in an envelope addressed to my mother all these years ago, and then when I woke up in hospital not knowing who or what I was, it had gone,' said Albie. 'Goodness knows what happened to it.'

'But we know your mother got the letter. Will told us,' said Jack, scratching his ear. 'She followed all your instructions.'

'Yes, but I didn't have time to tell her what to do with a dead man's heart. She probably fed it to the . . . hate to say it . . . pigs!' snapped Albie, flicking marauding snakes aside with his wooden stick shaped like a finger. He shouted half-heartedly, 'O Rerek, I am protected by . . .' and then finished, 'Oh, never mind. What on earth's the point?'

But at the mention of a dead man, Jack's gaze turned to the corpse of Will Waite, now dangling in an un-dignified scarecrow-like fashion from either side of the tomb, forming a useful bridge for those beetles who hadn't already fallen foul of Blackie and his friends. 'Wee Willie Winkie Waite,' he said slowly.

Albie looked positively green. 'I know. I'm so sorry, brother.'

'No,' said Jack, excited. 'Don't you see? They changed their name to mean something. We. Will. Waite. Albie, your name was . . .'

'Albert Cornthwaite.'

'And so your mother was Vera Cornthwaite, beloved wife, mother, B-C chapel organist?' He'd even seen her

314

hanging around the graveyard. 'Tight curly grey hair? Anxious expression?'

'Correct.'

And Jack practically barked with delight. 'I know where the heart is!'

He waved his arms around to part the swirling gases. 'Set up the scales again,' he signalled under his breath. 'Keep the tomb clear. We're going to have to be quick, or we're all pig feed.' Seth's open maw now surrounded them like a ring around Saturn, and beetles were beginning to fling themselves lovingly into the fiery hole, egged on by the antenna-waving Moonshiner.

Albie and Minty stared at each other above Jack's head as he crouched down low, whispered, 'Sorry, dead people,' and then pictured his destination.

Rather to his disgust, he sank straight through Granny Dazzle's sarcophagus, landing knee deep in her bandage-wrapped left arm. Then, mostly at ground level and so fast he couldn't be seen, half in and half out of the floor, Jack whizzed out of the crypt and into the graveyard. The next second he was beneath the ground, his head reeling from the overpowering smell of garlic from the coffin he was in. Vera had obviously thought the monster who would one day appear might be a vampire. Jack shrugged. Couldn't really blame her. He'd thought it too for a while.

'William Cornthwaite, you did a fine job of mummifying your mummy,' said Jack. The bandaged body was liberally sprinkled in amulets and brooches, and Vera wore a mask that was startlingly lifelike, right down to the halo of silver curls that framed her face. Jack tapped it gently. 'Plaster of Paris,' he said, nodding approvingly.

Alongside the mummy was a little row of jars, each with a different animal head on the lid. Jack dropped a hand through the earth he was standing in (another advantage of his god-like status, he supposed), rummaged a bit and pulled out Lord Jay's journal. '"Canopic jars",' he read. '"Falcon head . . . intestines." Human head has the liver. Monkey? No, baboon. That's the lungs. And Jackal – hello, my friend – is Duamutef who looks after the stomach. And the heart was the only organ to remain in the body.'

Jack turned over Vera Cornthwaite's hand. 'So what, then, are you holding, Mrs Cornthwaite?'

It could have been a mummified potato, judging by the size of it, but Jack knew exactly what it was. With a respectful nod to the mummy, Jack imagined the top of Granny Dazzle's sarcophagus and zoomed backwards towards his friends.

He was just in time, and that was only if he'd guessed correctly. The whole of the crypt was more or less swamped in snakes and beetles and slime from the top down, while flames raced up the walls to meet the foul gunge halfway. Albie and Minty were fighting off whatever they could, but the force of the onslaught was wearing them out. The ghosts were in a worse state still, and had completely given up, floating around the perimeter of the room like wisps of burning candy floss.

'Now!' yelled Jack, rising up through the plaque on top of the tomb, already unwrapping the bandaged object in his hand. It had to be as light as possible. Finally the heart fell from the last shred of wrapping into his other hand, perilously close to the hideous breath of Seth. 'Get away, you evil pig,' murmured Jack. Then he nodded to Albie.

Albie slid the scales to his feet.

Jack nodded to Minty. She laid the Feather of Ma'at on the bouncing bronze pan.

Then Jack knelt down and gently placed Lord Jay's

317

mummified heart on the other side. The scales tipped and swung, and Jack held his breath. From what he knew of Lord Jay, he'd been fond of gambling and drinking, hunting and releasing ancient gods from their bindings. Maybe his heart wasn't that true after all . . .

The scales began to settle. The feather was lighter. No, heavier. No, no, lighter. The waiting was agony, and just as Jack was about to add a hefty hand to the feather side to tip it down, he looked up to find that they had an audience, and a great span of eagle wings was spread, ready to suffocate them, the angered, horrified face of Gouldian Finch roaring, with his piggy eyes rolling in their sockets . . .

Clunk.

The Feather of Ma'at in its bronze pan grazed the tombstone, once, twice and then finally came to rest.

'Yes!' hollered Jack. 'Lighter!'

Then he wrapped Granny Dazzle's necklace around the heart, and threw it up in the air. 'Two true hearts beat as one. Eat that, pig-face!'

Flames roared around them as Gouldian Finch exploded with rage, and beetles scattered and burst open in every direction. The vast shelled body of Wormwood Moonshiner scuttled up Will Waite's back, trying to leap up to join his partner in crime, but slipped and fell on to the second bronze dish of Jack's scales. They tipped alarmingly and then crashed down on to the side of the beetle.

'Heavy!' yelled Jack, and no sooner had the word left his canine jaws than the wall to the crypt from the graveyard split completely asunder, and a creature more terrifying than even the pig-headed Seth appeared, with the snapping jaws of a crocodile-head mounted on the serpentine, sinewy body of a lion and ending in the bone-crushing rear end of a hippopotamus. It was so huge it could have eaten all of them in one neat mouthful, but instead, as Jack and Albie fell back on to the floor in terror, the creature followed Minty's pointing hand, honed in on the scrambling cat-sized beetle and wolfed it down in a gulp. Then, as quickly as it had appeared, it withdrew.

'What the heck was that?' gasped Jack.

Albie ran a handkerchief over his sweating fore-head. 'That, my dear Jack, was Ammut the Devourer.'

And Jack was even more relieved then that the hearts of his great-grandparents had been light. True and light. And there they were, true and light, shimmering col-umns of radiance that raced towards each other from

319

opposite ends of the crypt, Lord Jay beaming from beneath his ridiculous moustache, and Granny Dazzle, well . . . dazzling, thought Jack with a sob. She was as she had been on her wedding day – young, beautiful, happy. With a smile so beguiling she could possibly have stopped Ammut the Devourer in her tracks, she turned to Jack and nodded, tears glistening in her eyes. Then she glanced at Albie, who kept turning his head from one to the other of them, not knowing where to look first, tears in his eyes too, and she blew him a kiss which he caught self-consciously in his handkerchief. And then, like a flame in a draught, they were gone.

Sighing, Jack remembered another pair who'd needed help. He looked up. 'Ozzy'n'Ice, are you OK?'

Ozzy beamed down from the magic camp bed. 'We are OK.'

'OK we are!' shouted Ice from the other end. Between them lay the bundled body of an eagle, contained by the same enchanted bonds with which Gouldian Finch had ensnared Ozzy.

'You got him! Impressive.'

The camp bed descended to the floor. 'This is just the physical embodiment of his ba. Seth is still at large – it is not easy to entrap him. But we can keep this embodiment safely in our sights so it cannot prey on you again.'

'Good enough for me,' said Jack with a grin. The curse would be lifted. He wouldn't be a dog! Although there were certain parts of it he'd miss. But when he held his hands up to his head, he could still feel fur. Pointy ears. A long muzzle. 'Ohhhh,' he groaned. 'I'm still a dog-head.'

Albie stared down at himself too. 'And I am still . . . young.'

'I'm still going to kill you at basketball,' said Minty West.

But Jack bounded up on to the tomb, on a level with Ozzy. 'But why? I thought the curse would be lifted and my dog-head would disappear.'

Ozzy and Ice regarded each other with their hypnotic eyes, and nodded gravely. 'Seth is not thwarted, and you still must serve. You are Anubis. Your job is not finished.'

'Finished it is not.'

Minty yawned. 'Hurry up – I've got to go.' The hawk on her skull shifted restlessly as Mr Guisely sat up groggily in the corner of the crypt, stared at Jack and Minty, then collapsed in a heap again.

Peering through the open door at the graveyard, packed with hopeful-looking ghosts, Jack tutted. There was an awful lot of weighing to be done. 'I'll be here all night.'

'Probably,' said Albie.

'But at least if we do this properly we can muck up Seth's plans a bit . . .'

'Correct,' said Albie with a tight smile. 'And I, of course, will still be serving you anyway . . .' He didn't look too cross about it, and went to the door to usher in the spirit of Percy the gardener. But as soon as he stepped outside Albie's step faltered, and when he turned to look back at Jack in consternation his skin was white, his hair vanished, his eyes violet. Outside the crypt, he was Bone.

'Come back in!' shouted Jack, and he was delighted when Albie reappeared.

Which made him think . . .

He ran outside, feeling already that the fur on his face was receding. He touched his forehead gingerly. Two eyebrows! Then he sniffed the air. Nothing. Come the morning, he'd get lost the second he turned a new corner.

But when he stepped back into the crypt he could

see by Albie's expression that his dog-head had re-turned. 'OK,' he said mildly. 'In this crypt where I've got a job to do, I'm Anubis. Outside, I'm Jack. I can live with that, Albie the Bone.'

'And I can just . . . live,' said Albie.

Jack cocked his head. 'Was that a joke?'

'I never joke.'

Jack laughed. They could work on that. Every night, in the crypt, for the rest of their lives, for all he knew. And maybe even longer than that.

41

Jack woke to a distressingly loud alarm in his ear. For a second he thought he must still have his dog-head and his canine hearing, but then he discovered that his mother was standing at the end of the bed, shouting into the megaphone through which she had just amplified his clock.

'Get up! Get up now! People will be arriving in less than an hour, if anyone actually shows up at all. Out of bed.'

Furtively Jack scratched the end of his nose. It took a while for his hand to reach it, to his relief, and when his fingers made contact, they met with warm dry flesh, not damp quivering nostrils.

'Mother,' he said, jumping out of bed, 'I am up, and I'm going to help. Honestly,' he added when she looked at him in surprise. 'Expect lots of people.'

Doghead and Albie had cooked up the plot between them, but it was Jack who had tidied the museum, with a little help from Ozzy and Ice, and Bone and Minty who had driven Mr Guisely to the front steps of the Hampshire Media Group – radio, TV and newspaper – leaving him babbling incoherently about haunted crypts and possessed animals, with some murky photos on his mobile phone (taken by Ice) as proof.

Sure enough, the weekend news drew huge crowds, and Lady Bootle-Cadogan could barely contain her glee when Jack offered to take the first tour group, leading them straight into Lady Diselda's beautifully preserved quarters, through the museum and down the tunnel to the crypt. All Bone had to do was pop out at intervals in his old bandages, and the crowds were whipped up to a frenzy of delighted terror.

'What the godfathers was that?' ranted Lord Bootle-Cadogan, storming out of his office as Bone lurched across the corridor, moaning copiously. 'Bone, is that you? Oh!' He stopped, finding himself the object of close inspection by a group of Japanese tourists who'd never seen a real lord before. 'Morning. Er . . . *KONICHIWA*,' he roared, bobbing like an emu.

Jack gave him a thumbs-up and drew the crowd

down to the gift shop. The tours kept him busy all day, and given the night he'd had he would have expected to be more tired. But the look of pride on his mother's face and the relief on his father's were enough to keep him energized.

All weekend the tourists ebbed and flowed, until finally Monday morning came around and Bone entered at 7.30 a.m. to wake him as usual.

Jack plodded down to breakfast, not knowing quite what to expect. His mother beamed at him. 'Off to school then, darling? You all do so well there.'

That could only mean one thing. 'You're not . . . not sending me to Eton?'

'Well, perhaps one day,' said his father from behind the newspaper.

'But right now we do think that school of yours must be doing something right.' His mother walked the length of the table to drop a kiss on the top of his head. 'That marvellous performance over the weekend. And some *nice* friends waiting for you in the vestibule this morning.'

Jack stared at her, then at his father, then at Bone, who busied himself behind the cereal boxes. He was obviously going to have to find out for himself. 'Bone, can I have a lift?' he said as he left the room. 'Five minutes?'

'Sir,' croaked Bone obediently.

Jack waited until the corridor was completely clear of early-morning National Heritage people, and then sprinted down it. It felt good to run. Hall-Running – back to normal.

At the door were Minty West and someone else. Jack pushed open the door, and Fraser the basketball player grinned sheepishly at him. 'All right, Posh?' said Minty with a sniff. 'Fraser wanted to see where you lived.'

'I did not!' said Fraser, looking even more uncomfortable. 'That makes me sound terrible. No, I just wanted to congratulate you on running that Comp course in a mask. You should totally have won. Made my day that did – the look on Guisely's face. And I wondered . . . well, if you've ever considered joining the basketball team. You're tall and you're fast. I'm sure we can teach you to catch without bursting the ball.'

Jack gaped at him, and Fraser obviously took it as a no. 'I've told Minty to lay off you, I promise,' he said.

Jack grinned at them both. 'I can handle Minty. And Guisely.'

'You're in then?'

He could hardly believe it himself, but . . . 'Yeah, OK,' he said casually. 'I'm in.'

It was the best day of his life. Later, as they worked their way methodically through the patient souls waiting to head off to the Field of Rushes, Jack and Bone (as Doghead and Albie) dissected the whole of the last week in minuscule detail.

'One thing I don't follow, old man,' said Albie. 'How did you know where Lord Jay's heart was?'

Jack laughed again, pulling his ghetto blaster from under the altar. 'Do you remember I had to use this at Granny Dazzle's funeral? I've been staring at that gravestone for days, wondering what was wrong with it: VERA CORNTHWAITE, BELOVED WIFE, MOTHER, B-C CHAPEL ORGANIST.'

Albie studied it from afar. 'Cornthwaite not Waite?'

'No. There isn't an organ in the chapel,' said Jack. 'Never was, never will be. So she had to mean a different type of organ. The heart type.'

And he smiled at the ghost of clever Vera Cornthwaite, humming Barry Manilow's *Copacabana* gently to himself.

'That's a terrible song,' groaned Albie. 'I'm sure Fraser and those cool people you're becoming so fond of wouldn't sing it. You're not normal, Jack Algernon Bootle-Cadogan.'

And Jack's canine-toothed grin got even broader.

A selected list of titles available from Macmillan Children's Books

The prices shown below are correct at the time of going to press. However, Macmillan Publishers reserves the right to show new retail prices on covers, which may differ from those previously advertised.

Jill Marshall

Jane Blonde, Sensational Spylet	978-0-330-43814-8	£5.99
Jane Blonde Spies Trouble	978-0-330-43825-4	£5.99
Jane Blonde, Twice the Spylet	978-0-330-44657-0	£5.99
Jane Blonde, Spylet on Ice	978-0-330-44658-7	£5.99
Jane Blonde, Goldenspy	978-0-230-53244-1	£5.99
Jane Blonde, Spy in the Sky	978-0-330-45812-2	£5.99
Jane Blonde, Spylets Are Forever	978-0-330-45813-9	£5.99

All Pan Macmillan titles can be ordered from our website, www.panmacmillan.com, or from your local bookshop and are also available by post from:

Bookpost, PO Box 29, Douglas, Isle of Man IM99 1BQ
Credit cards accepted. For details:
Telephone: 01624 677237
Fax: 01624 670923
Email: bookshop@enterprise.net
www.bookpost.co.uk

Free postage and packing in the United Kingdom